her spy at dawn
book four, spy games

PAULA
ALTENBURG

This book is a work of fiction. The characters, incidents, and dialogue are drawn from the author's imagination and are not real. Any resemblance to actual events or persons, living or dead, is entirely coincidental.

Published by Paula Altenburg
Stewiacke, Nova Scotia Canada
B0N 2J0

Copyright© 2017 by Paula Altenburg
Cover design by Syd Gill/Syd Gill Designs
Interior formatting by Author E.M.S.
Edited by Amanda Bidnall, PhD

ISBN: 978-0-9937166-6-9
www.paulaaltenburg.com

Printed in the U.S.A.

"International intrigue, adversaries with more in common than they want to admit, and ohhhh the chemistry...I couldn't put HER SPY TO HAVE down!" ~Samanthe Beck, *USA Today* Bestselling Author of *Emergency Engagement*

"Sex, spies and video-tape... if you like your characters hot and your stories smart, don't miss this great read!" ~Roxanne Snopek, *USA Today* Bestselling Author of *The Chocolate Cure* on HER SPY TO HOLD

"HIS SPY AT NIGHT by Paula Altenburg is an intriguing and engrossing entry into the author's spy novel series. Readers will be enthralled by this latest selection." ~ Judge, *Writer's Digest 4th Annual Self-Published e-Book Awards*

From *Her Spy at Dawn*:

He dug in his heels at the bedroom door, jerking them both to a halt. He caught her arm, pulling her against him. He tipped his head to the side as he studied her face. "I thought you wanted to play?"

She did, but saw no reason to tell him how much. It might scare him off. "That depends. Exactly what kind of games are you into these days?"

Light fingers burrowed under her hair, cupping the back of her neck. A thumb rolled across her bottom lip. "How far are you willing to go to find out? How much control are you willing to give me?"

He was testing her. He used to call her Miss Bossy Pants for a reason. They'd had a great sex life, but they'd both been inexperienced and she'd called all the shots. He was letting her know that tonight things were going to be different.

She looked forward to it. "Your wish is my command—on the condition that, whatever you do to me, I get to do to you."

A slow smile began to spread across his face, flowing upward from his lips to his eyes. Meanwhile, for her, heat shot in an entirely different direction. He could have her right here, up against the door frame, if he gave the word. She wanted him *now*.

"Some of it might be anatomically impossible because we're working with different plumbing," he said, "but I get your point. You've got a deal."

CHAPTER ONE

AT QUARTER PAST SIX on a cold Tuesday evening, Dan Hanson pushed through the heavy wood-and-brass door of the Greasy Weasel.

Stale beer stench and warm body heat slammed Dan in the face. He unrolled the fleece collar of his black leather flight jacket and tugged down the zipper as the door swung closed behind him. The small pub, situated on a low-traffic side street off ByWard Market in the center of downtown Ottawa, was relatively quiet at this time of day. The working crowd was on its way home, and the evening hockey fans—those who couldn't get their hands on tickets for the Canadian Tire Centre—hadn't yet settled in. Dan hoped to catch the game between the Penguins and the Senators on the pub's big screen after his meeting. Sidney Crosby, the Penguins captain, was a popular Canadian player, but the Senators on home ice trumped a homeboy, and the match promised to be a good one.

He scanned the dim room and spotted John Carmichael, the Canadian Security Intelligence Service director, sitting in a corner with his back to the wall. It was the seat Dan would have preferred, because it offered an unfettered view of the dank room. But in this instance, he was OK with giving it up. John could be trusted to act as the lookout. He'd spent more than twenty years as a field officer, which had to be some kind of record. The Weasel had the added security of being owned by a former intelligence officer with an excellent grasp of his trade—past and present. Dan slid into the wooden chair on John's left, which gave him a view almost as good.

His boss looked tired. John was in his mid-sixties, not ready for retirement but far enough along in his career that the excitement was gone. Standing about the same height as Dan, he was thin without being scrawny, and even in a pub chair in a low-brow drinking establishment, he appeared dignified and relaxed—two looks Dan could never pull off. John had fastened a portable audio scrambler to the underside of the table. Dan could see the tips of the clips used to hook it in place. If anyone tried to listen in on their meeting, they'd be disappointed.

John wanted this meeting kept as far off the record as possible. CSIS had been chasing intel on the Canadian Minister of National Defence for almost two years now, and they were close to nailing him to the wall.

"Marlies is on her way," John said as Dan signaled to the bartender for beer. "Her flight got in this afternoon."

Marlies Wiersma—Lies, pronounced *Lees*, to the people who knew her well—was a CSIS intelligence officer who'd just spent several months in the Netherlands gathering information on Canada's current defense minister, Patrick MacKenzie. Normally she answered to Dan, who was her team leader, but because the case involved a sitting cabinet minister, John had insisted that no written reports be submitted and that all intelligence go directly to him. No one wanted the defense minister tipped off that he was being investigated by CSIS.

This would be Dan's first briefing on whatever Lies had unearthed, and he hoped it was good. Seeing the smug bastard's face on television piously preaching about Canada's duty as an international peacekeeper left his blood boiling.

"You're going to lose her," John was saying. "I wanted you to know before she gets here, in case she mentions it."

"Lies? She's being assigned a new team leader?" Dan couldn't hide his surprise, or possibly, a tiny twinge of hurt. He liked Lies, even if she did have a gigantic feminist chip on her shoulder.

Maybe that was why she was being reassigned. He wasn't always as politically correct as he could be— although he found it hard to believe she'd complained instead of coming to him first. It simply wasn't her style.

"You could put it that way." John wrestled a faint smile. "The aerospace and defense trade commissioner to the Netherlands has requested she be permanently assigned to his personal staff."

"Son of a bitch."

John lost the match with his grin. "I told him yes, but with certain strings attached. She has to be available to me when I need an extra person in Europe."

By *person*, John meant *woman*. Women made good intelligence gatherers because both male and female targets often shared confidences they wouldn't with men.

And by *permanently assigned*, the trade commissioner meant that he and Lies were sleeping together and the arrangement was serious. Dan knew the two of them were involved because Lies had possessed enough sense to give him a heads-up, but damn, he hated to lose her. Kudos to her, though, for refusing to give up her career. The trade commissioner, apparently, wasn't a fan of it.

"Harry's a good guy," John said. "And now he owes me. I view this as a win-win situation."

Harry Jordan was a rising star in international diplomatic circles, so yes, having him in the CSIS director's debt was a coup. Dan wondered if the poor SOB knew what getting involved with Lies was about to cost him.

No doubt he did. And Lies would be worth it.

The door of the Greasy Weasel opened to let in another blast of chilly air and a long-legged, stunning blonde dressed all in black. Flakes of snow clung to the sleeves of her woolen pea coat and she paused in the doorway long enough to brush them from her hair. The move was a calculated one. She'd be committing every face in the room to memory, because she was here on secret business and someone else might be too.

Lies Wiersma possessed the bouncy curls of Shirley Temple and the same blue eyes as a collectible doll Dan's sister owned. She was at least two inches taller than his five-foot-eight frame. Thigh-high leather boots added an additional three inches. Depending on the image she wished to present, she could pass for a professor, professional athlete, or some 1920s mob boss's brainless moll. She made an excellent intelligence officer precisely because she was a chameleon, and Dan was about to lose her. Why couldn't Harry Jordan keep his hands to himself?

Heads turned as she crossed the room.

"Hey," she said cheerily, plopping her pretty ass in the chair beside John and across the table from Dan. The table jiggled as she swung her long legs beneath it, and the toe of her boot caught its pedestal. John rescued his drink before it could spill. Her already rosy cheeks pinkened. "Whoops. Sorry about that."

There was nothing pretentious about her—another reason Dan liked having her on his team. She faked artless better than sophisticated, simply because it suited her personality.

The bartender brought him his beer, and Dan ordered another for Lies. She requested a Guinness. "To counteract all the wine I'm forced to consume at embassy functions," she explained. She added a dramatic sigh for effect.

"Your life is so rough."

Dan tried to sound sympathetic. Part of him was. He had zero interest in fancy events. His background in intelligence had involved survival in third-world conditions. He'd take the third world any day. The thought of having to wear a tuxedo ranked up there with performing emergency open-heart surgery on a dining room table during a firestorm.

"Just keeping it real."

The three of them chatted about the weather until Lies had her drink in front of her and the bartender returned to his station.

Then they got down to business.

"Lies, why don't you walk Dan through your report?" John said.

She gave him a briefing, clipped and precise. The defense minister had close personal friends who'd been running decommissioned Canadian weapons systems parts—used aircraft parts—through various maintenance companies in Europe. From there they made their way to nuclear-capable countries that Canada didn't do military business with because they hadn't signed the Nuclear Non-Proliferation Treaty. Several of those countries had uneasy relationships with their neighbors.

"The sales are arranged by a Canadian lawyer named

Mike Freeland. Payment and delivery are made through dummy corporations managed by Bernard Vanderloord, a Canadian ex-pat with dual Dutch citizenship. Both Freeland and Vanderloord went to university with the minister, where they became good friends," Lies explained. "After university, Vanderloord began an export business roughly based on a hawala system of exchange, leveraging off his and his friends' familial connections in foreign countries. Freeland's family is Ukrainian on his mother's side. Vanderloord has improved and expanded his business over time."

In a hawala system, an agent in one country—usually connected to the client through family or community—arranged for payment in another country in cash, goods, or services of equal value. It was a system based on reciprocity and trust. And it was illegal in Canada, as well as in most member countries of the United Nations.

Unfortunately, it was also incredibly difficult to shut down. Canada's money exchange laws remained pitifully easy to circumnavigate. All one needed were the right connections and colossal cojones.

Patrick MacKenzie had both in spades.

Dan sipped at his beer. There was more to the story than Lies was aware. An officer in Thailand had first uncovered the Dutch-Canadian connection while chasing military parts thefts that passed through maintenance companies in Asia. The officer's intel had led to the Dutch *Politie* and Interpol arresting another Canadian ex-pat named Marc Leon Beausejour. While Beausejour remained uncooperative, he too had been a good university friend of MacKenzie's.

A second intelligence officer had found a connection between the Russian Business Network—a cybercrime organization with links to the Russian Mafia—and the defense minister's office in Ottawa. Vanderloord also had connections to the Russian Mafia.

All roads lead to Rome.

"Thank you, Marlies," John said. "When are you returning to the Netherlands?"

"I'm packing up my apartment and giving the landlord my notice. I'm hoping to book a flight out for Sunday," she replied.

Intelligence officers tended to live light, keeping very few personal possessions. Besides clothes, Lies wasn't high maintenance. Harry was a lucky, lucky man. If Lies had been five inches shorter and not on his staff, Dan might have made a play for her himself.

She drained her beer. "You gentlemen have things to discuss, and I have packing to do." She yawned. "Not to mention the six-hour time change is doing me in."

"Give my best to Harry," John said.

The pub was filling up as hockey fans trickled in, rowdy and ready to drink. Staff maneuvered between tables, holding aloft precariously balanced trays of drinks. Lies, smiling at everyone she encountered and exuding an enviable glow of contentment, declined several requests to join tables on her trip to the door.

The aerospace and defense trade commissioner was good for her. And to her. The evidence of it was plain. Dan was happy for her. He didn't know Harry Jordan, but what the hell. He was happy for him too.

It was the world he felt sad for.

The noise level provided great cover. John and Dan leaned in closer, two casual friends waiting for the game to begin.

"Lies didn't give us enough information to take down a sitting member of Parliament," Dan said.

"There's more. She wired Vanderloord's Amsterdam

apartment and got some fantastic intel," John said. "She had to send it to me to get it translated. On a recent business trip to the Netherlands, Freeland brokered a sale of military parts to the Ukraine. Vanderloord arranged for payment through one of his companies."

What John had tasked Lies to do was illegal—but only if he got caught, which was unlikely. CSIS was a civilian organization that turned the security intelligence it gathered over to the appropriate law enforcement agencies as it deemed necessary. Since CSIS never gave up its sources, its methods couldn't be questioned. The onus was on law enforcement to make any intel they received stand up in court.

"What's the next step?" Dan asked.

"I've called in the Public Prosecution Services of Canada and requested an RCMP investigator. We both know it's not guaranteed that MacKenzie will go to jail, but his arrest might apply enough pressure to make him give up his supply chain and information on how far it extends."

That supply chain was CSIS's real objective. Canada's national security came first. Dan, however, wasn't about to endanger any member of his team. "Are you sure we can protect Lies?"

"I hope so." John frowned and met Dan's eyes. "Vanderloord found the wire she planted. Right now he believes Harry's behind it, but if MacKenzie talks to him about the evidence against him, Vanderloord is going to put two and two together and figure out where it came from. If that happens, Marlies's career as an intelligence officer will be over, and I might not be able to protect her from prosecution. She'll wear this alone." His jaw was set, his quiet voice determined. "We're not going to allow that to happen."

Dan knew what had to be done, but he didn't like it. "So the next step is to make sure MacKenzie and Vanderloord don't have that conversation."

"You still have your contacts?"

Dan had worked deep undercover, with some of the best people in the world in the worst of its places. After things went to shit for him in Sudan, he'd gotten out. He'd never lost touch with his friends, though. They'd do anything for him. He'd do the same for them. No questions asked.

"I do," Dan said. "I hate this," he added. *Hated* it. The noise in the room, so welcome only a few moments ago, now scraped against his eardrums.

But he'd do it, and John knew he would.

"If you liked it, I wouldn't ask it of you. Besides, there's no need to contact them right away. Let's give it a few months until after the investigator is finished examining all the evidence. It'll be months before charges are laid, and I want time to get Harry and Lies out of the Netherlands first." John ordered two more beers and set them both in front of Dan. It was now quarter to eight. "You going to be able to sleep tonight?"

"Should I be able to?"

"Yes." John said it with no hesitation.

"Then I'll be fine." Dan trusted his boss as much as he trusted anyone he hadn't worked with in the field. They all had occupational hazards to deal with and tough decisions to make. It was the way of the world. His world, at least.

"Good. We meet with the RCMP investigator tomorrow morning at seven o'clock in my office." John gave the table a final pat as he stood to take his leave. "Enjoy the game."

Yes, well. It was too late for that. He didn't touch the

beers John bought him, but left them sitting on the table throughout the game.

Alcohol wasn't how he chose to deal with moral dilemmas.

Dan strode through John's open office door the next morning, hangover-free and with a black coffee in hand.

It was eleven minutes to seven, and he wanted to be in place ahead of the RCMP investigator. It would give CSIS a psychological advantage by showing he and John as a united front. CSIS planned to cooperate as much as possible, especially since they'd called this meeting, but the Royal Canadian Mounted Police, the federal and national police force, were sticklers when it came to points of law. Months—years—of hard work, not to mention lives, could be destroyed by a single misstep on the part of either organization, so exchanging information turned into a careful game of poker with no one willing to reveal too many cards.

Dan and John spent a few minutes discussing the game. The Senators had won it in overtime. At six minutes to seven, the phone rang. The security desk downstairs had a guest waiting, and John, because his executive assistant hadn't yet arrived for work, had to go down to sign him in.

Dan watched the snow fall outside the office window and sipped his coffee while he waited for John to return. Ottawa was settling into winter and the streets were a mess of slippery, dirty slush. A car slid into an intersection, causing a traffic jam at the lights. Horns blared.

He heard voices in the hall and turned away from the drama unfolding outside. He rose from his chair to greet the investigator, setting his coffee mug on John's desk.

The investigator turned out to be a woman, not a man. John ushered her into his office ahead of him, the silly smile on his face telling Dan she was charming and pretty. She was small, maybe five foot two, slender, and wore practical winter boots instead of the office heels women seemed to prefer—which made sense because of the weather. Her hooded coat was bright, royal-blue serge and she'd wrapped a white knitted scarf around her neck to fill in any gaps. She had her head turned away from him, saying something to John over her shoulder. Straight shiny hair, a rich shade of cherry-brown red, spiked Dan's interest. He had a weakness for gingers. Especially the dainty ones.

However, something about the tone of her voice sounded an alarm in his head. A memory twigged. His heart started to race even before he could place it. She turned to him as John began to make the introductions and stretched out her hand. Both of them froze. Wide blue eyes trimmed with thick black lashes—which he knew for a fact were naturally reddish brown—met his. They reflected his horror.

John's voice came at him as if from the bottom of a long, echoing chasm. "Dan, this is Alycia Evers, the investigator the Public Prosecution Services sent over. Alycia, Dan Hanson. One of our team leaders."

Dan couldn't force his heart rate back to normal. He'd have to wait for it to settle all on its own. Hopefully that happened before he threw up or passed out.

"We've met," he managed to say, and was proud the words came out normal. At least he hoped they did. The dull roar in his ears made it difficult to be certain. "Alycia and I went to the same university."

"It's been a long time since Dalhousie," she replied, recovering faster than he did. "I haven't seen you in what—nine years?"

She knew exactly how long it had been, probably right down to the hour and the minute. And she hadn't seen him at university. It was at a funeral. The memory of that awful day was indelibly imprinted on his brain. He could recall every detail of the visitation room—who'd been around her, what she'd been wearing, the stark expression of loss deadening her eyes. Roses had covered the plain casket behind her. To this day, Dan couldn't stand the sight or smell of them.

I begged him not to go, she'd said to him, as if she couldn't quite figure out where things had gone wrong. *But he said you'd let him know if there was any real danger.*

That was Terry—too trusting, right up to the end. Dan had warned him before he signed on as a volunteer doctor that Sudan was unstable, but Terry had believed in the best of human nature. He'd probably thanked the bastards who'd taken his hospital staff hostage, and then slit his throat when Canada wouldn't negotiate for their release.

And Dan... Rather than offering her words of comfort, as inadequate as they would've been, he had done his job. He'd been searching for clues about the events behind that hostage taking. Information. *Think, Allie. Can you remember what Terry said to you last? What was his last phone call to you about?*

She'd looked in his eyes and she'd *known*.

"Has it been that long?" Dan said, pushing the memories away. The coffee twisted and turned in his stomach. "Wow. Look at you. Working for Public Prosecution."

She'd wanted to be a lawyer. Between them, she and Terry had planned to save the world. Dan had been out of step with them and their philosophies. He was all for saving the world too, but sometimes a hammer was needed.

"I work for the RCMP," Alycia corrected him. "The DoJ has oversight."

She was a cop.

Dan hadn't pictured that. Not at all. He'd thought she'd end up doing something for Human Rights.

John appeared reconciled to letting them take a mutual stroll down memory lane for old times' sake, but Dan had no intentions of going there. Besides, the whole point of this early meeting was to avoid drawing unwanted attention to it. No need to prolong it.

"We should get started," he said.

He helped Alycia with her coat and scarf, hanging them on the rack behind the office door while she dug through her briefcase and he got his bearings. She used a pen and paper to take notes, he saw with approval. Good for her. That couldn't be hacked—or accessed by anyone with an equal or higher security clearance.

As John laid out the facts of the intelligence CSIS had gathered, Dan studied Alycia. A plain navy suit jacket and skirt and a white blouse with a frilly collar screamed feminine practicality. No rings on her finger. Her only jewelry was a fine gold chain with a solitaire diamond pendant and matching diamond studs, a set that she'd inherited from her grandmother when she turned twenty-one. The color combination of blue eyes and red hair was natural, even if she'd darkened her hair, and her smooth, creamy skin remained as flawless as ever. She'd always been fussy about sunscreen. No freckles for her.

God, she was gorgeous. A lump of regret jammed in his throat, but he worked it free. He'd been the one to break up with her. A year later she'd begun dating his best friend. The two of them were much better suited.

Or they had been. Terry was dead. Best not to forget it.

Alycia began asking questions about the chain of events surrounding their case against the defense minister. John answered. Occasionally, Dan was consulted to fill in a few blanks, a reminder that this was a business meeting. Slowly, as he listened to John and Alycia, he got over his shock. His pounding heart no longer threatened to burst from his chest. However hard this was for him, for Alycia it had to be a thousand times worse, and yet no one would guess.

The Alycia he'd known wouldn't have hesitated to show the entire world what she was feeling. She'd been all fire. Now she was ice.

"I'm going to need your sources in order to conduct a proper investigation," she said. Her hair flipped a little where it met her shoulders, dynamic red against don't-mess-with-me blue.

"You know I can't give them to you," John replied.

Of course she knew that. It didn't mean she wouldn't do her best to get them.

"Unofficially, then."

"Not even unofficially, I'm afraid."

She was just warming up. "We're talking about taking down a sitting Member of Parliament. If we're to be successful, I'll need everything."

Dan admired her approach. She was using the *we* word, placing the RCMP, the PPSC, and CSIS all on the same team. They were and they weren't.

"I've given you all that you need," John countered.

"It's up to the RCMP to confirm its veracity and build a legal case against MacKenzie."

She tapped her pen on her notepad. "Not giving me your sources will leave the Public Prosecution Services and the office of the Judge Advocate General with the impression that CSIS overstepped itself when gathering this intelligence. Let's not forget Global Affairs Canada."

The GAC handled Canada's foreign relationships. This crap was complicated. Another reason Dan preferred fieldwork.

"I have complete faith in you and your investigative abilities as we move forward together on this," John assured her, turning her own tactics against her. "Your boss sang your praises, so it seems unlikely we'll need to worry about any impression the PPSC forms. As for the JAG's office, I'm sure you can handle them too."

Alycia's cheeks dimpled. "You have a lot of confidence in me considering this is the first time we've met."

John didn't have dimples, but his answering smile was equally charming. "I run CSIS," he reminded her. "I did my homework. This isn't your first investigation of a government official."

"Maybe not," she conceded, "but this one is a lot higher up the food chain, and it goes well beyond expense account fraud." She tucked her notepad into her briefcase. "Why don't we all think on what our next steps will be, then meet again in two weeks' time?"

"Perfect." John slid a business card across his desk toward her. It was simple, with only his name and phone number printed on it. "Call me directly when you're ready."

The business card followed the notepad into her briefcase.

Dan scrambled to get her coat. He held it for her as she stuck her arms in the sleeves. The soft scent of vanilla clung to her skin and he tried not to breathe in too deeply, even though he wanted to inhale it into his lungs and let the memory of it override the smell of roses attached to her that he couldn't seem to shake.

"Why don't you walk Alycia down to the front desk and sign her out for me?" John said to him.

His brain hadn't yet fully recovered from the shock, so he couldn't think of a way to decline. She didn't look enthusiastic either.

They were silent as they walked to the elevator. She had no more to say than he did. The past was the past. It was better off left alone.

When the elevator doors whispered shut she rounded on him, her eyes flashing with the blue sapphire flames he remembered. "Doesn't it bother you at all that if you don't give me your sources to work with, Patrick MacKenzie might well get away with murder?"

Yes. And she knew exactly how much it bothered him.

"That's a little dramatic," Dan said.

"You don't call it murder when he's supplying military weapons systems parts to hostile nations and they're dropping bombs on innocent people?"

The elevator hit the ground floor. The doors opened. Civil service workers were beginning to arrive for their day shifts while others were finished their nights. There were a million things he would've loved to say in his own defense, but in the end, she was right. She was also wrong. MacKenzie was only one part of a much bigger problem.

He remembered the reason why they'd broken up all those years ago. He'd been recruited by CSIS, and at the time her world was so filled with do-gooding she would never have understood the work he'd chosen to do. He'd hoped someday she might.

He'd gambled and lost.

"It would be murder even if the people weren't innocent," he replied, taking the wind from her sails.

He stepped back to allow her to exit the elevator first. As they got off, others got on, thankfully ending the conversation. He signed her out at the front desk and waited while she turned in her visitor pass.

He offered her his hand. Hers was small and warm. Familiar and not. Then he uttered the second biggest lie of his life—and he'd told a lot of them.

"It was great seeing you again," he said. "I look forward to working with you."

He watched as she headed out the main doors and passed through the front gate onto the street. The snow was falling heavier now. She disappeared into a squall of white flakes—a slim figure in a royal-blue coat, one gloved hand holding her hood over her red hair to fend off the approaching storm.

CHAPTER TWO

ALYCIA HAD BEEN LOBBED a hand grenade with the pin already pulled. Did she toss it away, or did she hold her thumb on the detonator and hope for the best?

She hailed a cab. The storm was gathering steam and she wasn't walking. She gave the driver the address for her condo. She'd work from home for the day rather than drive to her office at RCMP National Headquarters. The cab's passenger seat window had already crusted over with snow and was steaming up so that the city passing by was a blur of shadows and light. The streets were a mess, and she wasn't much better.

Seeing Dan Hanson again had proven she wasn't as over the past as she'd believed herself to be. She couldn't say which pained her more—the memories of Terry, who she'd loved with all her heart, or of Dan, who she'd loved and hated in equal measure.

The two men, best friends from the time they were nine or ten, had made an odd pair, at least on the surface. Physically, they were polar opposites. Dan was lean and dark, and while taller than Alycia—everyone was—on the short side for a man. Terry had been big and blond. Friendly to a fault, he'd genuinely liked people. They liked him too, children especially. He'd gone into medicine and then pediatrics, the perfect occupation for him.

She'd met Dan first and fallen for him hard. The six months they'd been together were impossible to forget. He'd been quiet. Calm. So fascinatingly intense. Whenever he turned that intensity on her, she'd felt like the center of the universe. She'd never quite been able to figure him out, and the mystery had driven her crazy.

Terry, on the other hand… He was the shoulder she'd cried on after Dan dumped her. They'd become friends. Then, a year after she and Dan broke up, Terry had kissed her. She'd offered him plenty of signals before, but she suspected he'd consulted Dan first.

That Dan had given his permission, and passed her on like a discarded toy, still left her burning with rage. She'd been nothing to him—or at least, far less than he'd been to her.

What she'd shared with Terry had been slower to build, true, but deeper and equally intense. Losing Dan had been hard, but Terry's death, and the circumstances around it, had almost destroyed her. For months after the funeral, which to this day she couldn't remember in any great detail, she'd operated in a daze. No one but her—and possibly Dan—had understood Terry's reasons for heading into a war zone hostile toward foreigners. In Terry's mind, children were children the world over and he would do what he could to help them. He'd been this big, bright, shining star, and the world was a darker, sadder place for his loss. Hers certainly was. She didn't dare think about what his last moments must have been like. If she did she'd slide back into the abyss. She didn't know if she could find her way out a second time.

Seeing Dan brought everything back.

The cab stopped in front of her building. She handed the driver a twenty over the back of the seat, pushed open the rear door, and stumbled into a blast of wind-driven ice that stung her cheeks. Her boots skidded in the slush created by the salt scattered on the partially cleared brick walkway.

Once inside, the soothing silence of the familiar glass and marble foyer greeted her. She gripped her keys in one hand and her briefcase in the other as she took the elevator to her condo on the twenty-first floor. From there she sent a message to her assistant, telling her that she'd be at home for the rest of the day.

She hung her damp outer clothes in a closet, put on a pot of coffee, and took her notes into the spare bedroom she'd converted into an office. The only guests who ever slept on the fold-out futon were friends from her university days or sometimes her sister. Her parents, Torontonians who hated to travel, opted for either the Westin or Fairmont when they grew tired of waiting for her to visit them. She booted up her Mac and settled in at her desk, checking her email while she sipped her coffee and pondered the mess John Carmichael had dumped in her lap. Snow and ice tickled the windows, the wind rattling the panes.

She spent the morning poring over the skinny file Carmichael had given her and researching federal acts, outlining which ones the case would fall under and how she'd address them.

When she finished, she tapped the end of her pen against her desk and watched the storm rage outside. It was midday, but the streetlights were on—pinpoints of flickering light in a swirling gray maelstrom. Patrick MacKenzie was guilty. No doubt in her mind about that. The problem was how to prove it. All she could take to a

PPSC special prosecutor was what would stand up in court. So far she had very little.

There would be no winning this case. Tackling it could well ruin her career. She was simply too junior, a David pitted against a Goliath. And yet she wasn't going to leave it alone. The thought of a cabinet minister—an *elected official*—getting away with murder, no matter how indirectly, ignited her moral outrage far more than the thievery and treason. She'd never be able to live with herself if she didn't at least give it a shot.

Her boss had known she'd feel this way. He'd also been aware that she had an ace up her sleeve, no doubt hoping she'd play it since the stakes were this high.

She picked up her phone and punched in a series of numbers with her thumb. "Hi. It's me. I need a favor."

The next afternoon, Alycia entered the office of the Director of Special Prosecutions in the PPSC National Headquarters. The storm had passed, leaving the sky a brilliant blue and the city a pristine oasis of fairytale white. Plows had been out all night and again this morning, clearing the streets.

It was impossible not to be glad to be alive on such a day. She'd learned to count her blessings.

A very tall, very thin woman with short, spiky gray hair tipped in blue came out from behind her desk to give Alycia a hug.

"It's so good to see you," she said. "It's been too long since we've had lunch."

Meredith Lively was Alycia's aunt on her mother's side. While taller than Alycia, her eyes were the same shade of blue and her hair had once been a comparable red. Meredith, focused on her career, had never married. Alycia and her sister Patrice were the closest she'd come to having daughters and she liked it that way.

"I've been busy," Alycia said without guilt, because her aunt was far busier than she was and understood the demands on her time. She sank into the plush leather guest chair facing the U-shaped mahogany desk. "Maybe we can fly to Toronto together for Christmas."

The two women chatted for a few moments about family and what they were doing before Meredith caught the time on her thick silver watch. "I love you, sweetheart, you know that, but I've got to be somewhere else in fifteen minutes. What's this favor you need?"

Alycia outlined the facts of the case she'd been handed.

By the time she was finished, a frown puckered Meredith's brow. "MacKenzie is popular. He's got a lot of high-powered friends in the House and the Senate." She was silent for a long time. "You were handed a case no one else would take because it can't be won," she finally continued, pointing out what Alycia already knew. "If you want my professional advice, it's to go back to CSIS and insist they give you their sources or the investigation is over. But even if they want to give them to you, which I guarantee you they won't, Global Affairs isn't going to allow it. It would mean admitting that CSIS spied on a Dutch citizen on Dutch soil—no matter that he's also Canadian—which could lead to an international incident. The Dutch aren't going to like that."

MacKenzie might be popular, but he was *guilty*. Yet her aunt made a good case against pursuing him.

"What would you do if you were in my shoes?" Alycia asked.

"If I were a young RCMP investigator eager to make a name for myself and willing to gamble with a few years of my career?" Meredith pressed her palms together and clapped her fingers, thinking out loud. She lifted one eyebrow, a slender smile curling the corners of her lips. Mischief gleamed in her eyes. "I'd go to the director of Special Prosecutions and ask her to handpick me a prosecutor who'd go after the case like a pit bull. I'd circumvent every rule—without breaking any laws, mind you—and I'd call in every favor I could think of to get my case into court. And I'd harass my liaison at CSIS until he or she gives up their sources, whether I can use them or not, because in my heart and my soul, I'd want to know that their information is solid."

Alycia wished she could say that any information Dan provided her with would be as solid as a rock, but she couldn't. She didn't know him anymore. She hadn't really known him eleven years ago, either. If she had, his desertion wouldn't have caught her so completely off-guard.

She needed his sources.

"What if CSIS won't give them up?" she asked.

Her aunt spun her chair away from her desk, signaling that the fifteen minutes were up. She and Alycia both stood.

She patted her niece's arm. "They won't. That's how we always know when their intelligence officers are doing things they shouldn't. Which is why I'm going to assign you a pit bull who'll cover your backside. And also why you've got to make sure your own conscience is clear. If you do choose to pursue this, it's going to get very complicated and ugly."

At the door, she gave Alycia a final hug and one parting piece of advice.

"Whatever you do, don't trust our friends over at CSIS. They might deal in information, but how they get it, and what they do with it, is all a big game to them."

Mid-afternoon, Alycia thumb-dialed the handwritten number on the back of the plain business card John Carmichael had given her. Her hand shook, but only a little, when Dan answered the phone.

"Hanson," he barked, terse and efficient.

"It's Alycia." She cleared her throat and tried to match her tone to his. "I'd like to meet for coffee."

She could practically hear his hesitation rumbling down the connection. "Where and when?"

She clutched the phone tighter, her persuasive argument dying on her lips, not as prepared for his acceptance as she should have been. She'd thought he'd refuse. "How about now? At the National Gallery café?"

On a late winter afternoon not too long before Christmas, they'd have the place almost to themselves. But it was public. Too public for personal conversations about the past. She was a crier, unable to hold back her emotions, and he'd always hated that.

She wasn't going to ask him questions about Terry, or what had happened in Sudan, or if anyone had been made to pay. It was over and done with, and time to move on.

"I'll meet you in the café in a half hour," Dan said, then hung up without so much as a good-bye.

She stared at the dead phone. What had she seen in him?

By the time she'd parked and made her way to the café, Dan was waiting for her at one of the round tables.

Normally she loved the bright and airy room with its large windows and unimpeded view of the city. Dan's brooding presence, however, made the space darken and shrink. She couldn't say why. At first glance he was average. There was nothing eye-catching about him. He wasn't a large man, maybe five feet eight at the most, although her own hours at the gym told her his lean build translated to wiry muscle. He had nicely-cut brown hair and cool hazel eyes. A faint five o'clock shadow scruffed up his image.

A second look, however, told a far different tale. Despite the casual office attire of dark dress pants, sage-colored shirt, and matching tie, he was a throwback to an earlier era, a man who could pass for a nineteenth-century gunfighter. All he needed were the holster and pistols. If the zombie apocalypse ever struck, she'd want him on her team. He held himself very still, as if in a permanent state of high alert. His gaze constantly scanned his surroundings, missing very little. He'd taken a seat that gave him an unimpeded view of the room and the street outside, a position she didn't doubt was deliberate.

The pulse at the base of her throat began to throb. Her lower lip quivered in a spontaneous chain reaction, and she bit the inside to hold it steady, trying to hide her dismay that she still found him so sexy.

Although his head never moved, his eyes followed her as she walked toward him.

Instead of *hello,* she blurted out, "What do you take in your coffee?" when she got to the table, fumbling in her purse for her wallet to give her hands something to do.

His chair legs scraped against the floor as he stood up. "Forget the coffee. We've got an hour before the gallery closes. Let's take a walk through the temporary exhibit instead."

The exhibit was empty. One person was on his way out

as they made their way in. They didn't bother to check their coats. Dan carried his over his arm.

"Wow," Dan said, his gaze lighting on a contorted bust of hammered bronze and papier maché. "It seems twentieth-century modern art is not my thing." Those intense hazel eyes swiveled to her face, so close to hers that she could see the green flecks around the pupils, and for a moment, she forgot how to breathe. "What did you want to discuss?"

She was direct by nature. It would do her no good to be anything else with him. They were both trained to read body language, and he'd be far better at it than she was.

Did you know rebel militants were going to storm Terry's hospital? Did you warn him? Did you tell him to get out?

Terry had trusted him. Why couldn't she?

"You have to convince John to give me your sources," she said.

Dan bent forward to read a display label. "He's my boss. I'm not his. He calls the shots."

"I promise they won't go any farther than me."

He moved on to the next display, his footsteps loud in the empty room, but his attention was on her and their conversation. She could feel it. This interest in art was his way of buying time to think before speaking.

"You can't make me any such a promise," he said. "Not one that will stick. You work for the police and Public Prosecution. At the end of the day, if your bosses start demanding answers from you, you're going to tell them anything they want to know."

She didn't react. She simply moved on to her next question. "Was any of your information gathered in the Netherlands?"

"I can't answer that."

"Tell me more about the Ukrainian connection, then." That was at least one snippet of useful information CSIS had given her, and she intended to pursue it first because it originated right here in Canada and she could get a court order easily enough.

He stopped in front of a display featuring a headless cloth doll and a plaque that read *Marie Antoinette*. "A lawyer named Mike Freeland was in the Netherlands on a trade mission back in early October. They were investigating shipbuilding opportunities for the new government contract that's out. He and the other trade mission members attended a helicopter trade show in Amsterdam while they were there. That in itself isn't unusual. The ships Canada is commissioning will require landing capabilities for helicopters. But Freeland's meeting with Ukrainian contractors was out of the ordinary—as was the Ukrainians' subsequent purchase of CP140 aircraft parts brokered through a Dutch-Canadian businessman. Ships generally don't require enough landing space for long-range patrol planes. And you already know that Canada is wary of selling parts for aircraft with weapons capabilities when they could end up helping to arm hostile nations."

"The Dutch-Canadian businessman would be Bernard Vanderloord, also a friend of MacKenzie's," she guessed.

Dan took her coat from her, ignoring her polite show of resistance, and draped it over his arm so that he carried both. "What's the next step in your investigation?" he asked.

"The Public Prosecution Services will assign a special prosecutor who'll work with me to make the final decision on whether there's enough information to press charges. So you can see why having your sources to verify what you're telling me is so important."

"My sources' lives are important too. So is their ability to move around in secrecy. Revealing who they are defeats the purpose of having a spy agency."

His elbow brushed her arm as he eased between two display pedestals. She doggedly pursued him, ignoring her raw nerve endings overreacting to the brief physical contact. "I could take the date of that helicopter conference in Amsterdam, check the list of Canadian attendees, and start cross-referencing those names against a database shared with Interpol. It would take time, but I'd find your officer eventually."

Dan actually laughed. Fine lines crinkled at the corners of his eyes. "I like to think we're better than that."

Heat pooled in her belly, turning her insides to mush, at the sound of his laughter and the memories it evoked. It was so rare, and yet so completely genuine whenever he let it out. The one honest thing about him.

Hearing it now, and feeling the effect it had on her after all these years, left her unable to breathe. She should have been unaffected. She'd gotten over him. She'd recovered. It was Terry who had owned her heart, and who did to this day.

Big, wonderful, stupid, trusting Terry, who'd been the second love of her life to have dreams more important to him than her.

"I've got to go," she choked out, averting her face. The tears she'd planned to avoid sprang to her eyes before she could stop them. She grabbed for her coat hooked over Dan's arm and played tug-of-war when it wouldn't come free. The door to the exhibit looked a long way off. The room started to spin. Everything was distorted, as if she were viewing it through the bottom of a glass. Her chest was on fire and her ears began ringing. "It's a woman thing."

That would keep him at a distance.

She was wrong. Instead he took charge, his smile wiped away by concern. "How did you get here?" When she told him she'd driven, he bundled her into her coat and ushered her out of the exhibit, his left arm braced behind her before she could blink. "Where are you parked?"

She mumbled the location.

The blast of cold air that met them when they stepped into the underground parking garage should have helped. When it didn't, her muddled brain figured out what was happening. She was having a panic attack. They'd hit her at odd times for months after the funeral, usually in the middle of the night when she couldn't sleep, but she hadn't had one in years.

Dan took her purse from her. "I hope you don't have anything too personal in here because I'm going to search for your keys."

He found the electronic fob on the first try and stuck it in his pocket. Then he passed her a crumpled tissue he'd also unearthed.

When they reached her car, she could breathe normally again.

"I'm fine," she insisted when he unlocked the doors of her Cadillac and pressed her into the passenger seat.

"Of course you are." He loped around the hood, opened the driver's door, and hopped in behind the wheel, playing with the seat to make room for his longer legs. "What's your address?"

She had no choice but to give it to him.

The drive took forever, thanks to a combination of icy streets, rush-hour traffic, and her silent mortification. She turned off her thoughts and focused on breathing slowly, the way she'd been taught. *One, two, three, four. Four, three, two, one.*

Dan stopped the car at the door of her condo's parking garage. "Think you can take it from here?"

She nodded.

He leaned a forearm against the steering wheel and regarded her with those eyes of his that saw everything. She read compassion and a kind of weary acceptance in them. "I'll talk to John in the morning about having someone else in the department assigned to the case."

Neither one of them moved. They continued to stare at each other.

She might never get another chance to uncover the truth. She needed to know. She'd been unable to uncover anything herself, but Dan was with CSIS. He'd been in the area at the time.

"You asked me questions at Terry's funeral," she said, clenching her fingers into fists so tight her knuckles ached. "You were investigating. Did you ever find out who his murderers were?"

CHAPTER THREE

DAN KNOCKED ON JOHN'S open office door. "Can I speak with you for a moment?"

"I always want to say no when people ask me that question." John set his pen down and adjusted his reading glasses so he could peer at Dan over the rims. "It usually means there's a problem."

"Not a big one. I want to withdraw from the defense minister's investigation."

John pointed to a chair. "Have a seat and tell me why."

Dan perched on the edge of the chair indicated. He cleared his throat. He'd practised for this moment all night, since he couldn't sleep anyway. Too many ghosts haunted him—ghosts of decisions he'd made and actions he'd taken.

"As you're aware, the RCMP investigator and I have a past," he began, his hands relaxed and resting between his knees. He might have practised, but it wasn't making this any easier. He'd never been big on sharing his feelings. "She's not handling having to work with me as well as I'd hoped."

His conscience kicked him for that. *Way to go, Dan. You coward. You just passed all the blame on to Alycia.*

John frowned. "What kind of past are we talking about?"

"She was engaged to a friend of mine who was volunteering as a doctor outside Darfur. Rebel soldiers took his hospital hostage. Three days later, after Canada made it clear we weren't prepared to negotiate, they used my friend to send Canada a message." Dan left it at that. There was no need to get into what they'd done to Terry's body.

"I know this story," John said. "I'm sorry for her loss. And yours. But I'm not sure what that's got to do with this investigation."

"I was working in the area at the time."

"I still don't see the connection."

Did he have to draw John a map? "She's asking questions about what I knew."

Did you ever find out who his murderers were? The hope and pain in her eyes, along with the remnants of the panic attack he'd caused, had cut to the quick. He'd hurt her enough. And he didn't want to be reminded of a decision he'd spent years trying to forget.

"Becoming more clear." John's expression shifted, ever so slightly, although to what, Dan couldn't say. "If she asks too many questions about it, you're to continue telling her you don't know anything."

"It's not as simple as that." Mentally, Dan forced his fingers to remain relaxed. "I was trying to track down any leads I could find regarding the hostage takers. I went to the funeral. I asked her what Terry said to her in their last phone calls."

"Did you have the authority to ask her those questions?"

"No."

He'd taken the initiative himself, seizing an

opportunity because it was there. He'd been so desperate to find Terry's killers, and with only two days off for the funeral, he'd pumped Alycia for information at a time when she could barely stand upright.

He'd been taken to task by his team leader for his rogue investigation too. That hospital had been full of children. The Americans had insisted nothing be done to jeopardize their safety and Canada agreed. The Sudanese soldiers had assumed Canadian doctors' lives would be worth more to the Americans and their allies than the children, and they'd been mistaken. The volunteers were on their own.

"But she believes you did," John said, finally getting it. "And now that she knows you're with CSIS, she also believes you have access to a whole lot of insider knowledge no one else would."

Dan wasn't about to admit that Alycia had known he was with CSIS from day one. When he'd signed on he'd been instructed not to discuss it, but he'd been in love and told her anyway. "I was going to say that I'm an ugly reminder of a past she'd rather forget."

John's frown deepened. "She didn't strike me as someone who forgets much of anything. *Tenacious* is the word that springs to mind."

"An even better reason for me to be removed. She's going to keep asking, and I don't have any answers. None she needs to hear." Finding Terry's killers had proven impossible. They would never have been held accountable anyway. The world wasn't that fair. He'd come to accept it.

And besides, that wasn't the real question she'd wanted to ask him. It was merely the key to the floodgate.

"I don't give a damn if working with you is difficult for an RCMP investigator," John said. "She's got her job to do, and at the end of the day, she's not my problem. My concern is that she's not the only one having difficulty dealing with the past. That problem does fall back on me." He studied Dan, who fought hard not to show how desperate he was to have this case reassigned.

"My answer is no. My advice, however, is that you two work this out between you somehow."

As much as Dan didn't want to take John's advice, if he wasn't going to be reassigned, he had no choice.

But he wasn't doing this in public. That had been Alycia's initial mistake—to think they could avoid the past as long as they weren't really alone.

He called her that night.

"How did you get this number?" she demanded. Her annoyance pulsed through the connection. "It's unlisted."

The question told him she was rattled. "How do you think I got it?"

It took her a second. When she figured it out, she sounded more pissed, if possible. "I'm a *police* officer. I don't care if you're CSIS. You don't get to break the law whenever it suits you."

"Relax. Your assistant gave it to me."

"She did not. She'd never do that." Alycia said it with just enough doubt, however, to acknowledge the possibility existed.

He leaned against the wall in his kitchen, the cell phone pressed to his ear. Through the window in the door he could see the neighbor's Doberman bounding through the snow in his back yard. Again, despite two polite requests that the dog crap in its owner's bushes, not his.

"Believe whatever you want. All I know is, when I told her I was the PPSC lawyer assigned to a confidential case you're working on, she couldn't give me the number fast enough."

"My God. Some things never change. You're still the world's biggest liar."

"I wouldn't say I'm the world's best. That's a pretty bold claim."

"I said biggest."

"Biggest, best... What's the difference?" Dan countered, enjoying himself more than he should.

"Saying best might suggest I condone it, which I don't. From now on, stay out of restricted databases," she advised him. "At least while you're part of this investigation. Don't make me report you."

"There'd be nothing for you to report."

He knew how to cover his footprints. Tracing them would be a waste of money and resources, and she wouldn't bother, because the end result would be the same. He'd continue to have unrestricted access to government databases. And they'd still have to talk.

"If this is about what happened at the art gallery, I'm fine. I got a little light-headed. All I needed was something to eat."

He wasn't the only liar in this conversation. "You asked me a question and I didn't answer. You deserve an explanation, but not on the phone. Can I come over?"

He could hear her take a slow, measured breath, then hold it in before letting it go along with her garbled answer. "I don't think that's wise. It's late. You were right. The past can't be changed. I should leave it alone and focus on the investigation instead."

The Alycia he knew had been into karate, tackling opponents twice her size in competition. She'd challenged professors. One of his friends had led a tutorial for a course she'd taken and he'd been afraid of her. John had captured her perfectly when he'd called her tenacious. She never left anything alone.

This Alycia, the one who suffered panic attacks even after nine years, made him smell roses again.

The Doberman in his back yard finished its business and headed for home, bounding through snowdrifts. That was what Dan was about to do—take a crap in Alycia's yard. "Maybe it isn't wise, but I'll be there in forty-five minutes."

The night was cold, crisp, and clear, the streets bare for the first time in days, and traffic was light so he made good time. He currently owned a fixer-upper in a small suburban community fifteen miles from downtown Ottawa. Flipping houses was a hobby of his. Fixing cars was another. He drove an old Volvo he'd picked up for parts, then decided to rebuild it instead, because except for a few spots of rust he'd sanded out and filled in, the body was sound.

Most days though, he took public transit to work. City parking was a pain, and he liked having the time to read his morning paper and listen to music. Except for the harmless, crazy former professor who recited poetry and solved complicated physics equations out loud—free education for the teens—the other passengers were ordinary, daily reminders that good people outnumbered the bad. It gave his work added value.

Alycia buzzed him into the building.

As he looked around he could only imagine what it cost her to live here. More than he earned, anyway. Her family had money—her dad was some fancy-ass Toronto architect who designed luxury homes for the rich and famous. It was one of the many differences between them, although in fairness, the one time he'd gone home with her for a holiday dinner, the only one who'd felt the difference was him. Her family had been welcoming and gracious.

An older couple passing through the foyer on their way out cast him side glances, as if wondering how he'd gotten in and whether they should call the cops. He didn't blame them. His flight jacket and jeans had seen better days, and it paid to be cautious.

Alycia answered the door as soon as he knocked.

She hadn't dressed to impress. She wore a pair of bright yellow yoga pants and a long-sleeved white cotton jersey, with mismatched fuzzy socks on her feet—one yellow, one white. She'd pulled her cherry-brown hair into a stick-straight ponytail. Direct blue eyes peered up at him from a face scrubbed clean of makeup. Her eyelashes were red tonight, a shade lighter near the tips, rather than mascara black.

"You can come in," she said, sounding as if she didn't care one way or the other, but the hand she'd pressed to the base of her throat and the unblinking steadiness of her gaze told him a different story. So did the deliberate casualness of her clothing, because the last thing Alycia was—or used to be—was casual. She was on edge.

All of which relaxed him, lifting a great weight from his shoulders. She was better prepared to protect herself tonight. There'd be no more panic attacks. No tears.

No smell of roses.

Thank God.

He stepped across the threshold and entered her condo. Bold oil canvases filled the walls of the entry. When they were dating, she'd begun collecting original works from promising art students. He'd lost count of how many galleries he browsed, more interested in her than her hobby, stupidly happy to bask in her enthusiasm as she chatted with artists.

He took off his boots and followed her into the living room. More bright colors greeted him. An L-shaped purple sofa. Buttery yellow leather chairs. A navy rug under the glass coffee table. City lights dimpled close-drawn floor-to-ceiling curtains, adding an air of cozy warmth to the picture. The propane fireplace was on. The coffee table held a half-empty glass of red wine, a mostly full crystal decanter, and a second glass that he presumed was for him.

"Would you like a glass?" she asked, reaching for the decanter as he sank into one of the leather chairs.

"No thanks. I have to drive." Translation: *I won't be staying long.* He shouldn't be here to begin with, but he wanted to gauge her reaction while they talked.

The heating system hummed to life, jetting warm air into the room through a vent above his head. Now that he was here and they were alone, he had no idea how to proceed. Small talk was painful for him.

"I'm sorry I was an asshole at the funeral," he began.

"Were you? Honestly, I don't remember. We were all shaken. I doubt if anyone was at their best." She looked away as she spoke.

She remembered, all right.

"Maybe I will have that drink."

She filled the second glass and handed it to him. He held it but didn't taste it. He needed an object to focus on. A crutch. But alcohol wouldn't hold a story together.

She curled her feet under her, leaning against the armrest of the sofa, and took a sip of her wine before setting it on the end table beside her. Soft lamplight caught her hair. She certainly wasn't trying to impress him, but he preferred her this way.

"You knew Terry chose Sudan because you told him that's where you were working," she said.

The underlying accusation in her tone slid like a sharp blade between his ribs. He had. The two men had been out drinking. He'd finished his first assignment and wanted to brag a little about fantastic, important job and how much he loved it. Terry had wanted his reassurance that he was OK with Alycia and him. Dan wanted them to be happy. But together? He couldn't say yes for certain, and it ate at him to this day.

She held her clasped hands in her lap. The knuckles were white. Whatever was going on in her head, it didn't bode well for him. "He trusted you to tell him if there was going to be trouble in his area."

The blade twisted, prying his ribcage apart. Of course Terry had trusted him. "The entire area was unsettled. He knew that going in." He rolled the stem of the glass between his thumb and forefinger, wanting to get this over with and get out. "You asked if I ever found out who his killers were. I didn't. I'm sorry."

But again, that wasn't what she really wanted to ask him. He braced for tears or a fight. Possibly both.

She swallowed twice before she could find words. "Did you know his hospital was going to be attacked? Did you warn him, and he decided to stay anyway?"

The knife retracted, ceasing to twist. So that was her fear—that Terry had known, but chosen to ignore the danger. She was angry with Terry, not him. All he had to do was say yes, he'd warned him, or no, he'd known nothing. The temptation was there.

But he couldn't do it. Not to Terry, and certainly not to Alycia—who'd spent nine years blaming the wrong man, with no outlet for her anger.

So much for Dan and Alycia working things out between them.

"I knew," Dan admitted. "I was under strict orders not

to tell anyone. I was young, and new to intelligence work, so I didn't."

Tears welled behind her eyelids. She blinked them away. This Dan, who could calmly announce that he'd allowed his best friend to be murdered because he was following orders, was a man Alycia had never met.

There had to be more to the story.

He didn't offer any further explanation or try to justify his decision. He simply sat across from her holding a glass of wine he had no plans to drink. He'd taken off his coat, and it was scrunched up behind him, ready if he needed to make a speedy exit at the first opportunity. The dim lighting in the room didn't disguise the fine lines at the corners of his eyes or soften the sharp angles of his face. Neither did she miss the pain behind his carefully blank expression. Whatever the reason for his decision not to inform Terry, it hadn't been easy on him. He'd suffered.

Good.

And yet his confession generated an enormous amount of relief. It had tortured her to think of Terry knowing what was coming and doing nothing to save himself. Perhaps it was selfishness on her part, but the thought that he'd cared more about strangers than her had left her so angry with him. She wasn't transferring that crippling anger to Dan. She had enough reasons already to be angry with him.

"Under the circumstances, I'm sure your bosses will understand if you ask to be removed from the case," Dan continued, with enough hope to be insulting.

Was that what he thought? That she was too fragile to deal with the past?

She could see why her panic attack might have given him that impression, but it wasn't so. She'd just needed to *know*, and Dan was the only person who could give her the answer.

Now she had it.

She couldn't say how she felt about his disclosure. There were so many emotions surrounding those dark days, although their edges had been dulled by time. One piece of advice she'd received continued to guide her, however.

Life was for the living.

"Terry died nine years ago. It doesn't rule me. Besides"—and this was the clincher—"if I were to withdraw from the case, no one else would take it on."

"Why not?"

As if he didn't know. But she'd play his game. She preferred this topic of discussion to the one they'd begun with anyway. "If CSIS won't give up its sources, then it's by no means a sure win. I'll have to find real proof to support your intelligence. We're talking a months-long legal investigation against a man who is heavily connected, and I won't be able to take any action without the special prosecutor's approval first. That's a serious handicap."

He stretched his legs out, crossing his ankles. He'd left his boots by the door and she could see that the sole of one of his socks had worn thinner than the other.

"Then why haven't you turned it down?" he asked. "If we lose, it can't be good for your career either."

"It might set me back a few years," she admitted. "But imagine what it could do for me if we win."

She had another, better, reason. She hated to see

dishonest, selfish people get ahead when someone like Terry, who had been all about helping others, never received any benefits for the great things he did. He'd never get justice. It was her way of paying it forward.

Dan set his untouched glass of wine on the coffee table beside the decanter and planted his hands on his knees, as if preparing to stand. "Are we OK to be working together?"

She wouldn't say that. She had too many issues to slog through. A lot of her memories—the high points as well as the low—were connected to him. He'd broken her heart. He'd let his best friend down, regardless of his reasons and/or intentions. In her mind, the two men would be forever intertwined.

There *had* to be more to the story. The Dan she'd loved would never have allowed rules to stand in his way if his conscience dictated otherwise. He was about protecting the people closest to him. Did he think she didn't know why he dumped her?

Although bottom line, the biggest reason was because he hadn't loved her enough. And it bothered her that even today, despite everything, her stupid heart reacted to him. She'd thought that useless organ had flatlined a long time ago.

"Of course we're OK." She drained the last of her wine, untucked her feet from beneath her, and got up to place her empty glass next to his. She didn't know if there was a woman in his life, and she didn't want to know. "It's a shame you came all the way over here at this time of night rather than simply talking to me on the phone. You could have saved yourself the trouble."

They were standing, the table between them.

He zipped up his leather jacket and thrust his hands in the pockets. "I had nothing better to do."

"That's not the least bit insulting."

"It wasn't meant to be."

He grinned and her knees turned to jelly. The ice between them was broken. She could hear the cracks as it shattered, the tense muscles in her neck releasing their death grip. She'd been so nervous.

The grin faded. "Look, Alycia. Let's not lose sight of what's important. Let's do our best to make sure MacKenzie goes to jail. Not only is he greedy, he's a traitor. Selling out the military is treason."

"Only if it can be proven."

Dan rolled his shoulders, tipping his head side to side as if loosening up for a fight.

"Then I say let's prove it."

CHAPTER FOUR

"NONE."

The bald response was the RCMP assistant commissioner's estimate of how much information about its sources Alycia could get out of CSIS.

Alycia was meeting with her superior and the special prosecutor, David Williams, in one of the boardrooms at RCMP National Headquarters. David was tall and thin with black-framed glasses he was constantly pushing up the bridge of his nose with a finger. His middle finger. He had a somber and deceptively mild presence about him, and looked to be in his late twenties. Her aunt had assured her that looks were deceiving and he was a shark. He was also closer to forty years old.

Her boss, the assistant commissioner, had pale, disconcerting gray eyes and a steel-colored brush cut. His age was indeterminate. This was another instance where looks were deceiving. If Alycia didn't know him, and bumped into him on a deserted street late at night, she'd plant a heel in his groin, run for her life, and ask questions later.

"Global Affairs will fight to keep CSIS from giving up its sources," the commissioner continued. "We're involved in an international incident, but the GAC isn't about to let anyone admit it. How happy do you think the Dutch will be to find out that one of our ex-pats is conducting criminal activity on their soil and that Canada has been tracking him without their permission?" He addressed the special prosecutor. "How badly do you need those sources?"

David tapped the copy of the case file Alycia had handed him. "Based on this? I'd say about as much as my COPD grandmother needs her oxygen tank. CSIS has plenty of evidence, but a good lawyer will get ninety-nine percent of it dismissed."

Alycia's brain whirled, examining the situation from as many angles as she could envision. "Say we can't get a conviction. Can we at least ruin the minister's career?"

"Oh yeah." David said it with relish. "We disclose just enough evidence to keep the GAC from having a stroke, but that will also give the press something to sink their teeth into. And once the press gets a hate on for the defense minister, his career's over. *But*. And this is a big one." He adjusted the cuffs of his suit. "I'm not jeopardizing anyone's career—mine and yours included—just because John Carmichael says we can trust CSIS. While I'm sure his intelligence is sound, it's the methods used to acquire it that can be sketchy. My job is to uphold the law. If we're going to ruin a man's career, we want to make sure it's justified. I want to know everything CSIS knows, meaning I want to be better informed than the defense. If we have all the information, and can back it up to MacKenzie's lawyers without prejudice, then our hands are clean."

"Do you think you can get those sources if we make it clear they won't be disclosed in court?" the commissioner asked Alycia.

"Me? No." She shook her head. CSIS didn't trust the RCMP either. As she stared at David, however, a plan took form. CSIS had come to her. They wanted to prove the defense minister was guilty too. She and Dan had agreed to work together on this. To do that, he was going to have to give a little. "But our lawyer, on the other hand... David, you can talk to their representative, Dan Hanson, about how it's privileged information. Maybe cite client confidentiality. With the right approach, he might give it to you."

"What might the right approach be?" David asked.

She hesitated. Her conscience stirred. Did she really want to do this? Did she want to go down this path?

To unleash this monster?

Let's not lose sight of what's important.

"He and I go back a long way," she said. "I think I know the right motivation."

The assistant commissioner slapped his file folder closed. The meeting was over. "It's worth a shot. Alycia, you set up a private meeting between you two and the rep from CSIS. David, you can decide if we've got enough of a case against the defense minister to move forward and at least do some damage. We'll see how far we can take it."

Dan hated those rare days when he had to wear a business suit. It was the biggest downside to giving up fieldwork, although after two years at a desk, he'd learned to accept it as an occupational hazard.

It didn't take a genius to figure out why he'd been called to this meeting with the special prosecutor and

Alycia at the PPSC's national headquarters. They wanted CSIS's sources.

As he waited in the Public Prosecution Service's conference room, he focused on what he planned to say rather than the tightness of his tie. These were early days in the RCMP investigation. Too soon to send memos to other departments and give them a heads-up. CSIS knew how to keep secrets. His job now was to ensure that the RCMP and the PPSC didn't give the defense minister forewarning. He had an intelligence officer to protect.

At least the other night had cleared the air, and he and Alycia could look at each other again. All they had to do was get through this investigation and they could go their separate ways. Six months, tops.

She breezed into the room, a tiny, brisk bundle of energy, briefcase in hand. The sensible navy skirt and blazer, the white, buttoned-up blouse, and the practical navy pumps underlined that she was a force to be reckoned with. Those eyes, however…

Her lashes lowered, then widened. Icy blue irises shifted to the color of the warm waters of the South Atlantic when they lighted on him. Her full bottom lip stretched into a welcoming smile. She'd grown more beautiful than his memory recollected, and his recall for detail was good. He remembered how bright her smile was first thing in the morning, beaming at him from the pillow next to his. How it lit up the entire room in a way he could feel to the soles of his feet.

His gut clenched. He knew exactly what that look in her eyes meant. She was up to something.

And he wasn't going to like it.

The conference room door swung closed behind her.

"Hi, Dan," she said, taking the plush leather chair across the table from him, acting as if they were old friends and the eleven years since their break-up—or the nine years since Terry's murder—had never happened. His suspicions deepened. The other night hadn't cleared that much air.

The door opened again. A tall, bookish man with black-framed glasses and a thick file under his arm took a seat at the head of the table, with Alycia on his left and Dan on his right. His suit fit him better than Dan's did. Of course it would. It looked custom made, not off-the-rack.

And his interest in Alycia went beyond professional. While he did nothing to openly express it, Dan read it in the way he remained neutral toward her, giving her little more than a nod of his head to acknowledge her presence. With her extroverted personality and the warm smile she'd offered him first, she warranted more in a greeting than that. No normal man—woman either, since there was nothing sexual about it—would be able to resist smiling back without conscious effort.

Dan clenched his back teeth. Unbelievable. He was jealous.

Despite that, his overall first impression of David Williams was favorable. The special prosecutor made eye contact when he spoke. His handshake was firm. Once the introductions were over, he didn't waste time on pleasantries nobody gave a damn about but got straight down to business.

"CSIS did a remarkable job," Williams said, flipping open his file and shuffling the pages. Dan could see a number of sticky notes and page markers attached to them, which explained why the folder was so thick. "You people gathered a lot of intelligence."

Interesting. Dan was being sweet-talked, which meant Williams was up to something too. Had the RCMP and the PPSC joined forces against CSIS?

They ran through the details of the case again. The defense minister's involvement in military theft was first uncovered during an investigation of Marc Leon Beausejour, an ex-pat with shady international dealings, primarily in Asia. Further investigation revealed online security breaches using an electronic information exchange system through the Russian Business Network, a cybercrime organization specializing in identity theft. Finally, CSIS linked the minister to an illegal hawala bartering system run out of the Netherlands by an ex-pat named Bernard Vanderloord—which would drag Global Affairs into the mix.

Dan had no worries. If the RCMP and the PPSC had joined forces, fair enough. When it came to revealing its sources, Global Affairs would throw in with CSIS.

"You have enough on Bernard Vanderloord for a conviction. Why not pass this information to Interpol and let the Dutch investigate his connections?" Williams asked.

"The supply chain these guys have set up is pretty extensive," Dan explained. He wanted to steer the conversation away from Vanderloord. In light of his private conversation with John regarding the man's uncertain future, he didn't want Vanderloord and CSIS too closely connected in the special prosecutor's mind. "MacKenzie is only one link, whereas Vanderloord sits at the hub. If he goes down, everyone connected to him will disappear."

Williams slid his glasses up the bridge of his nose using his middle finger, letting Dan know without words what he thought of the explanation he'd been given. Nothing subtle about that. "I think we all know that CSIS only cares about the links in the chain that connect directly to Canada."

"MacKenzie is in a position of power and trust. He's

guilty of treason. Our men and women in the military deserve better from our leaders than this."

"They certainly do." Williams frowned into space.

The hairs on the back of Dan's neck prickled. He hadn't yet been asked for his sources, which he found suspicious. Williams, who'd been very direct on the surface, should have requested those first. And Alycia had been sitting too quietly, all of her attention on the special prosecutor, as if waiting for something that wouldn't be pleasant. Tension clung to her like a funky perfume.

"Would you say that innocent people could die from his actions?" Williams continued.

"I'd say they already have," Dan replied. No big revelation there. "If we don't take care of MacKenzie ourselves, it won't be long before the British and the Americans become involved."

"Then you can see why it's so important that our case against him be as strong as possible. As it is, it will never hold up in court." Williams had his palm on the file folder, his fingers splayed wide in a gesture of ownership. "If we want a conviction, I'll need your sources. Which you can give me under client/solicitor confidentiality, of course. Nothing will be on the record. I won't give any names to the court."

Like that put Dan's mind at ease. What did Williams think he was, a rookie? This wasn't his first rodeo. "What if the defense requests them and the court orders you to hand them over?"

"It won't come to that."

"It would take more than your word for me to risk releasing an intelligence officer's name. These people work undercover. Their lives are at stake. They trust me to protect them."

"Your officers understand the risks when they sign on.

They know what can happen when important information is withheld." He paused for a beat, then went in for the kill. "I would think you, more than anyone, would understand the importance of protecting the innocent."

Dan literally felt his heart stop, then lurch into overdrive as compensation. He glanced at Alycia, who looked away.

Enough of this bullshit. "If you've got a point to make, then make it."

"You were good friends with a Dr. Terry Nielson, who was murdered by militants in a hospital outside of Darfur in Sudan nearly ten years ago. You were in the area at the time and sat on intelligence that might have saved lives—his included."

Alycia sucked in a sharp breath. Her cheeks paled. "*David.*"

"He wanted honesty, Alycia. I'm giving it to him. I'd like some in return."

Williams was a lawyer doing his job. While Dan might not like his methods, he got it. But Williams had gotten that piece of classified information from somewhere, and it wasn't from him. At least not directly.

He shoved his chair away from the table with the backs of his legs. He didn't dare look at Alycia. She was an RCMP investigator. She should know better than this. What did she hope to accomplish?

Whatever it was, it felt kind of personal.

"It would have cost a great many more lives if I'd given it out," he said to Williams. "Terry, of all people, would have understood that. He would never have thanked me for releasing it either, even if it had saved him." He picked up his briefcase and crammed papers inside before snapping it closed. "I think we're done here for the day."

His overcoat hung on a rolling rack near the door. He grabbed it on his way out. The hangers rattled in protest at the abuse.

Alycia chased him into the hall. He heard her heels on the tiles.

"Dan! Stop."

She scooted past him to block his path. Her blue eyes, lashes fluttering, displayed remorse. He waited, stone-faced, for an apology he was too angry to accept. What she'd disclosed served as confirmation that he couldn't trust her with the names of those CSIS sources any more than he did the special prosecutor.

The apology never came.

"Terry might not have thanked you for it, but I would have," she said softly.

"Then you really don't get it, Allie," he replied, with equal softness. "Doing it for you wouldn't have made it right either."

Dan wrestled the sheet of Gyprock into place against the framed-in partition, and then, with his nail gun, fastened it down.

It was a Saturday night, but the dangling ceiling bulb cast a bright enough light for the job, which was a new kitchen. He'd torn out the old wall between it and the front room, making it bigger. He planned to turn the old dining room into a new living room. When he was finished, the house would be young-family-friendly and ready to flip. He liked to match renovations to the neighborhood, and the nearby elementary school made this one a no-brainer. The dark, ugly mudroom some previous owner had tacked onto the kitchen was coming off. He'd add a sunroom overlooking the backyard instead.

Then the new owners would have an unimpeded view of the neighbor's dog taking care of business in their hydrangeas. Something else he needed to fix.

He worked on the house most evenings and weekends. He knew he should work on a social life too, but his close friends were spread all over the world, and online dating wasn't for him. Besides, at any given time, night or day, one of his officers could call with a problem he'd have to deal with ASAP, and the classified nature of their investigations made that difficult to explain to new acquaintances.

So, after taking the desk job two years before, he'd learned to love his own company. The problem was that it gave him too much time to think. And for the past several nights, despite the hard physical labor, his thoughts had been hijacked by Alycia and a whole host of what-ifs.

He shot another nail home. When they were dating, he'd have done anything for her. That was one of the reasons he'd broken things off when he'd joined CSIS— he hadn't wanted or needed conflicting obligations. He'd been all about the blood-pumping excitement the job offered, but his days of chasing excitement were over. Dirty work ate at a man and made him question himself. There was a chance that someday he might need his soul.

If one good thing had come out of that meeting with the special prosecutor and Alycia, however, it was that he'd spoken the truth—Terry wouldn't have thanked him for endangering other lives. He'd heard his friend's voice in the back of his head, crystal clear, telling him to quit being a dumbass and focus on what was important. While the wounds of the past had been broken open and rubbed raw over the past few weeks, Dan had finally come to terms with his decision nine years before. He was ready to lay his conscience to rest, at least in that one regard. He'd done the right thing, regardless of his reasons.

What he couldn't figure out was how he felt about this new Alycia. Life had changed her. Him too, he supposed, because now that he was past the rush of anger over her giving out his private information, he understood she'd done what was needed to get the job done, and it wasn't as personal as he'd thought at first.

That was why it bugged him so much. He couldn't work with her when he couldn't trust her. She knew how to get to him in a way no one else did. He had to come up with some story to convince John of that.

Someone knocked on his front door.

He set down the nail gun, stepping over a stack of ceramic tile and through the framed-in partition for the new wall. One of his neighbors had been known to drop in on occasion out of good-hearted kindness and a side of nosiness regarding Dan's loner lifestyle. To be truthful, Dan didn't mind the idea of taking a break and sharing a few beers with another guy.

He slid back the deadbolt. The welcome died on his lips. Alycia stood on his doorstep, her shoulders hunched to her ears against the raw winter wind.

"How did you get my address?" was all Dan could think to ask as he wiped the Gyprock dust from his hands onto the thighs of his jeans.

A lock of hair swept across her mouth and stuck to her lips. She tugged it free with a kid-gloved finger. "John gave it to me."

Of course he had. "John should know better."

She looked so small, so ill at ease, that a spurt of

remorse lanced through his dismay. Then she got all snippy on him.

"You had no problem digging up my private, personal phone number, so now we're even. Can I come in?"

He opened his mouth to say no. To tell her that this time she was the one who should have called and saved herself the trip. But those words wouldn't form because he really liked women who stood up for themselves, and Alycia was an intriguing blend of softness and strength that never failed to sucker him in.

"OK. But the place is a mess."

He moved to the right to let her in, pressing his back to the wall and seeing the place as she would—the lime-green shag carpet, leather sofa and recliner, wallpaper in an orange psychedelic print, and big-screen TV. He wished he'd been a little farther along in the renovations, but at the end of the day it wouldn't have mattered. An old home intended for a mid-income family wasn't about to compare favorably with a downtown condo worth at least a million dollars.

He led the way to the kitchen. "I've got everything torn apart, but at least it's warmer in here."

He'd removed the painted plywood cupboards and put up temporary shelves beside the stove for basic cooking necessities. The counter and sink remained functional. He'd take those out last.

"I love what you've done with the place. It really makes a statement," she said, her cheeks dimpling as she took it all in.

She could be so freaking cute. "Yeah. It says 'bachelor.'"

"Are you?"

"Am I what?" Sitting at a desk must have made him slow, because he didn't understand what she was asking.

"A bachelor."

The question, while innocent enough, set off all kinds of unwanted feels. He kicked the cord to the nail gun out of her way with the toe of his safety boot. "What can I say? I'm set in my ways."

He found a chair that looked clean and placed it in the center of the room. Once Alycia was seated, he leaned against the counter. Beneath the glaring bare ceiling bulb, the setup looked like a bad made-for-TV interrogation scene. She unwound her scarf and unfastened her coat but didn't remove them, which was just as well. All he had to offer as host were instant coffee, beer, and some stale Oreo cookies.

"I didn't come here to apologize," she began.

"*A...a...and* we're off to a great start," he drawled.

That earned him one of her brain-addling smiles. "I'm trying to say that we have a common goal and should focus on that. I came here because I'd love for us to start over. Let's pretend we never knew each other before today. From now on, the past is the past."

Dan shook his head. "I can't pretend that." He held up a hand to keep her from interrupting. "But we aren't the same people anymore, so I do agree we should leave the past alone and try to start over. Otherwise working together is going to be too difficult, and neither one of us is in a position to walk away."

Those dimples winked at him again. "John said no when you asked to be reassigned, didn't he?"

He ignored the distracting dimples as well as the rhetorical question. He wasn't quite ready to start over just yet. "Before we agree to let bygones be bygones, I have a question for you." Her lower lip drooped. She wriggled in her chair, re-crossing her legs. He had to rein in a smile of his own. Once again he had the impression they were adversaries in a bad interrogation scene. "When you told David Williams about my past history with Terry, did you happen to mention yours to him too?"

She plucked at the tassels on one end of her scarf, all nonchalance. "No."

He pressed his advantage. Reason was his best defense against her. "Why was it OK to bring up my past but not yours?"

"Mine wasn't relevant to the situation."

"Mine wasn't either. What happened in Sudan has nothing to do with Patrick MacKenzie. Plus, my presence there is classified information."

"That was a long time ago," she protested. "There can't possibly be any harm in telling a special prosecutor about it now, especially under the circumstances."

"That's not your call to make. I'm a *spy*, Allie. I shouldn't have told you about it to begin with. The special prosecutor certainly has no business with the information, no matter how you try to justify it. That's two people who now know something they shouldn't. And three of us who should have known better."

She folded her arms across her chest. Her eyes locked with his. Her chin shot up in challenge. "Does this mean you're going to have to kill me?"

"And have the PPSC down my back for that too? No thanks. I'd be the prime suspect." He'd made his point. There was no need to belabor it.

She broke eye contact first, glancing at the floor as if in thought, then at her watch. "Let me make it up to you. I'll buy you dinner. We can discuss strategy—since you didn't like mine—and I can write it off as a business expense."

He was so tempted. But while they might want to put the past behind them, and he'd finally accepted that Terry wouldn't have sacrificed other lives in exchange for his, there was one thing he hadn't quite come to terms with— and that was his personal reasons for sitting on that information. He couldn't look himself in the eye and say with complete honesty that he'd held it back for the greater good.

While the dinner invitation was a definite temptation, getting too close to Alycia again felt a lot like profiting from the proceeds of crime. He'd had his chance and he'd blown it. They'd both moved on, and from what he'd seen, become better people for it. They were no longer young adults, wrapped up in themselves and each other.

"I'll take a raincheck," he said, ignoring the tiny pang of regret.

CHAPTER FIVE

ALYCIA COULDN'T EXPLAIN HOW Dan managed to look so ordinary and dangerous all at the same time, but he did.

The thighs of his well-broken-in jeans were coated in fine white drywall dust. He had more of the dust on the front of his shirt and in his brown hair. The faint workday scruff on his lean face had roughened into a Saturday night beard that would no doubt disappear come Monday morning. The gunslinger image he evoked reemerged. This was not a man to be messed with, yet that's what she was doing.

Inviting him to dinner?

Stupid.

Bringing up those CSIS sources right now would be another bad, bad idea and she wasn't that brave. While she didn't plan to apologize for doing her job or concede she might be in the wrong for revealing his personal history, she did want to make peace—and he wasn't making it easy for her.

He'd seized the position of power, offering her a chair while he remained standing, and even though she knew the trick well, it was effective in throwing her off her game. Besides, his point was valid. Not only had she not told David about her own connection to Terry, she hadn't mentioned how she'd known about Dan's.

But David had guessed when she'd walked back into the boardroom after Dan stormed out of their meeting.

"Is this going to require couples therapy to fix?" he'd inquired.

If she and Dan really did want to start over, then that might not be such a bad idea.

The kitchen was so warm the windows were steamed up and sweating. Dan had a space heater running, and she hadn't taken off her coat. The conversation was dying— her invitation to dinner, refused—and she had no more excuses to stick around. This was the weekend, and since he seemed determined to keep their relationship on a professional level, she was intruding on it.

And yet she wasn't ready to leave. She found him frustrating for all his contradictions. She couldn't figure him out. Despite being angry with her, or at least seriously annoyed, she could have sworn he'd considered accepting her invitation to dinner before turning it down.

"When did you develop this interest in do-it-yourself home renovations?" she asked.

"Right after I took the desk job and needed a place to live in that I could afford."

She wondered where he spent his paycheck. Although he hadn't come right out and said so, he'd insinuated he had no wife and children, past or present. His brother and sister were much older than he was, both already settled with good careers way back when he was in university, so it was unlikely they needed his handouts. His mom would be close to eighty by now, so there was that possibility, but she didn't think so.

That was the trouble with him—he'd always been too tight-lipped and distrustful of others. If he'd been more willing to include her in the decision-making process, they might have been able to make things work between them.

Or maybe he'd been right to call it quits. As an investigator who searched for truth carefully hidden between layers of deliberate subterfuge, she couldn't say she approved of his career choice. Not one hundred percent. And back in university, when she'd been all about finding a cause to support, her priorities would have chafed at him. He wasn't into public protests and waving placards.

This mystery was none of her business, and yet she couldn't let it go. "This isn't the kind of neighborhood where I'd expect you to live. Why did you buy a house here? Especially one that needs so much work?"

"To flip. The house itself is solid," he added. "I buy a place cheap, fix it up with as little investment as possible besides labor, and sell it as a starter home for a reasonable profit. It gives me something to do, plus I feel good about a young family moving into a decent place."

So Dan had a streak of altruism. She'd always known it was there.

"Can I give you a hand?" She looked around to see if there were some small task she might take on.

"Have you ever done any drywalling before?"

"No."

"Hung a ceiling?"

"Afraid not."

"Used a nail gun?"

"I'm a police officer," she reminded him, frustrated. "I've trained with a shotgun and I'm good with a nine millimeter. Do those count?"

A hint of a smile flashed in the depths of his hazel eyes, briefly touching his lips and stealing her breath before disappearing. "Not really."

"OK, I get it," she said, giving up. "You don't need my help." She'd run out of excuses to stall and it was becoming pathetic. He didn't want her around. She gathered her purse and her gloves. "We'll try another meeting with the special prosecutor sometime over the next few weeks. He wants to speak with the Prime Minister's Office first, then go over some of the details he flagged in your case file."

"I'll be available."

Dan walked her to the door. While neither of them was tall, and her boots had a decent heel to them, he had a few inches on her.

And, suddenly, she couldn't take it any longer. She hated him treating her this way—as if she were a stranger and he had to be polite to her. As if they didn't have a history together, no matter how rocky. They'd once *meant* something to each other, even if he'd been more to her than she was to him.

She set a gloved hand on his shoulder, rose on her toes, and placed a soft kiss on the corner of his mouth. His stubble prickled and instinctively she shifted her lips, sliding hers over his, creating fuller, deeper contact and giving the gesture more intimacy than she'd intended. It also lasted too long. Supercharged atoms ricocheted in the air between them, giving her goosebumps. Before common sense rocked her back on her heels, a string of sensations swarmed through her. Familiarity. Rightness. Opportunities lost.

The greatest, however, was shock. She'd meant the quick kiss to be a step up from the impersonal handshake he'd offered her in the CSIS director's office. She couldn't tear her eyes away from his face, watching the wheels turn in his head. She should have gone with a hug.

He didn't pretend she hadn't crossed an invisible line

as she'd half-hoped he might. Bleakness settled into his eyes. So did firmness. "Quit pushing me, Allie. Too much has happened. We're going to move forward. Not back." He reached around her and opened the door. "Let me know when you've got that meeting arranged. Drive safe."

She made her way down the icy walkway to her car, using her arms to help keep her balance and her pride to stave off humiliation. As she backed out of his narrow driveway she could see him slouched against the door jamb, arms folded, watching her leave as warm light spilled around his silhouette and onto the shadowed steps.

"Quit pushing me, Allie. Too much has happened. We're going to move forward. Not back." She was almost home before she thought of all the scathing responses she might have made to that—*Get over yourself, Hanson* primary among them. It was a simple kiss between old friends, not an attack on his virtue. She hadn't pushed anything.

And she hadn't been in it alone, either. He could have stopped, but he hadn't. She'd been the one to end it, not him.

She braked for a red light. The black Volvo beside her had a hole in its muffler that the owner enjoyed, if the sounds caused by him revving the engine were any indication. She frowned at the red BMW facing her across the empty intersection.

What did it mean that Dan hadn't ended the kiss first?

By the beginning of the work week she'd convinced herself it meant nothing other than that he was right. She had been pushing him, and yes, too much had happened. She had to be as much a reminder to him as he was to her of things best left behind them. Seeing each other again had shaken them both, but they could work through this. They could both be professional until this case was over.

If only he didn't make her so crazy. But until the PPSC got back to her, she had no reason to contact him. There was plenty of time to pull herself back together.

A month later, on a Tuesday, Alycia had lunch with David Williams to discuss their next steps.

The restaurant was one of her favorites, with secluded tables and a discreet staff who knew their lunchtime clientele. She and David finished their meals but kept their napkins on their laps, indicating to the waiter that their conversation was not to be interrupted.

"I think it's safe to say we can forget about CSIS giving up its sources," Alycia said. She didn't tell him that she'd gone to Dan's house in one last-ditch effort to reason with him, since it had gotten her nowhere.

"That's more or less what I expected after our last meeting with Mr. Hanson. We'll set it aside for now." David sipped at his glass of ice water. "I spoke with the PMO's office yesterday. Off the record, of course. The whole case is shaping into a political nightmare, which was also to be expected, but they've agreed there's enough evidence to proceed with laying charges. They're reviewing the information I gave them. Once that's done, we'll memo the Prime Minister." He tapped the water glass on the table, gently swirling its contents, his expression steady on her from behind the black-framed glasses. "You sure you're ready for this?"

Once they had the PM's approval there'd be no turning back. Word would be out. It would take less than two hours for the press to latch onto the story.

All she felt was excitement. She'd investigated a number of the dates and transactions CSIS had provided for the foreign exchange of military goods, and yes, they checked out. A commander at one of the Canadian Forces air bases was also now under investigation because he'd signed off on a significant number of the decommissioned parts that had been sold. So far an investigation of Mike Freeland, Patrick MacKenzie's lawyer, had yielded nothing, meaning the link back to the Minister of National Defence remained murky, but all it would take to bring him down was one verifiable piece of evidence.

Someone in that supply chain would break.

"Absolutely," she replied. "The defense minister is guilty."

"Based on the evidence we have, not necessarily what we can use," David reminded her. "Guilt doesn't always translate into a conviction. Don't ever forget that."

She might be a rookie when it came to her role as an RCMP investigator, but she'd been with the police force long enough to have experienced injustice firsthand more times than she cared to count. She didn't need them mansplained to her. "CSIS has MacKenzie in their crosshairs and that's a bad place for anyone to be. Including a cabinet minister. If they want a conviction, they'll find a way to make it stick."

David quit playing with the glass and folded his hands on the table next to his plate. "And I repeat—I have a problem with that."

"Because you don't like not knowing everything they do. You want your hands to be clean," Alycia recited. "Yes. I remember."

"That's not the only reason. What if we get too far into this and CSIS changes its mind? What if they suddenly decide a conviction doesn't fit in with their plans anymore?"

That would never happen. They wanted this. They'd come to *her*. "You're far too suspicious. Why would they do that?"

"They do it all the time. Information is a commodity to them. They make deals with other countries every day." David sighed. "I'm not being suspicious. I'm trying to be realistic. I'm looking for the risks. Like I said, we can move ahead on only a fraction of the information CSIS gave us. From what you've uncovered, that fraction is solid. But there's no room for error. I'm a really good lawyer, but all the defense minister needs is a better one, and believe me, his motivation to find one is going to be high. So although I'm confident in my abilities, I'd be more confident if I had greater faith in our team. If you get so much as the slightest hint that CSIS is losing interest or not being upfront with us about what they're really after, I want to be able to do damage control. Anything Dan Hanson tells you—*anything*—I want to know. We've already seen how willing he is to walk away if he doesn't want to give us an answer."

Guilt made her squirm. She was the reason David had gotten the impression that Dan was uncooperative. She hadn't provided all of the information—thereby illustrating the validity of David's argument.

"You took Dan by surprise," she said, suffocating her uneasy conscience by leaping to his defense.

"It would take a lot more than that to put an intelligence officer as experienced as he is off his game. I've worked with these guys before and I assure you, he gave me a carefully calculated response designed to leave me with the impression he wanted to make."

A sick feeling swelled in Alycia's stomach along with her guilt. Her lungs could no longer fully expand. Dan did know how to keep his thoughts to himself. When they were dating, she had no inkling that he'd applied to work for CSIS. Their breakup had come as a complete shock. And he'd only gotten better at lying.

Unfortunately for him, she'd also gotten better at exposing liars.

"I hear what you're saying." She placed her napkin beside her plate, smoothing the folds into place, signaling to the wait staff that it was safe for them to clear the table. "But if the Prime Minister's Office is in, then we're moving ahead. With or without cooperation from CSIS."

Dan closed his office door. He'd come from a debriefing with one of his officers in Belgium who'd been keeping an ear out for discord over CETA, the new free trade agreement between Canada and the European Union. Hostility ran high among its dissenters, both at home and abroad, and CSIS was monitoring the situation.

On his desk was a pink memo slip. Dan fingered the small piece of paper. Written on it was a phone number he'd committed to memory because of the number of times he'd longed to call it.

He'd been too harsh with Alycia. Ridiculously so. He could recall, in vivid detail, the shock on her face in response. But she'd already had a total meltdown over Terry thanks to him, and she didn't need more confusion and conflict to deal with. He shouldn't have allowed that kiss to happen. Certainly not to let it last as long as it did. Until he'd reminded her of it, she'd forgotten that they had a past, too. He'd given more than one intelligence officer a dressing down for unprofessional behavior on a case, and yet here he was, suddenly the worst offender. Why did he lose his mind around her?

Because he'd never stopped loving her. His heart was holding onto something that no longer existed. But it would let go, given time. He couldn't spend the rest of his life worrying what might trigger her next meltdown, or freaking out over roses. She'd be far better off without him.

Unfortunately, they couldn't avoid each other forever. He'd known this day was coming. The scribbled message beside the number was a request to set up a meeting. She'd be finished at least part of her investigation by now and wanting to go over more details before proceeding.

He wanted off this case, badly, but knew better than to ask John again. Emotional stability was crucial to a CSIS intelligence officer on the job, and he wasn't about to have anyone question his—not with his background in war zones. Especially since it wasn't his history he was most worried about.

Maybe avoiding the past was the wrong approach to take. Whereas he was pragmatic, Alycia tended to be hot-headed. Moving on was easier for him. Her personality type required closure. Maybe she needed to look back before she could go forward.

He picked up the phone.

She answered on the first ring, sounding crisp. Self-assured. Professional. That, he could deal with.

He responded in kind. "This is Dan. Returning your call. You wanted to set up a meeting?"

"Yes." He heard a rustling of papers, as if she were only half-paying attention to their conversation while she worked. "I met with the special prosecutor today. The PMO agrees we have enough information to lay charges. All we're waiting on now is the prime minister's green light. We should get together to discuss what will happen next."

Dan agreed. However, he wanted to meet somewhere private, so they could talk in greater depth and without the conversation derailing. But not somewhere as private as either of their homes. The memory of her lips beneath his had him shifting in his chair. There'd be no more of that either.

"How about I take you up on that raincheck for dinner? I'm buying," he added. That way he got to pick the location as well as take the lead in any discussion.

"I know a great place."

"So do I, Miss Bossy Pants." The old nickname slipped out and hung in the air. She loved to take charge, and he'd loved to let her—especially in bed. He closed his eyes and hurried on, giving her the address for the Greasy Weasel. "We can meet there at seven if that works for you."

"Charming name for a restaurant," she remarked with a deliberate lack of enthusiasm that left him grinning. He'd bet she hadn't seen the inside of a pub since her undergraduate days. "I'll bet the food is fan*tas*tic. See you at seven."

He was there a half hour before her, securing a secluded booth instead of a table and slipping a portable audio scrambler into place.

And then all he could do was wait.

He was reminded of their first date. The Lower Deck in Halifax, Nova Scotia, where a lot of Dalhousie students hung out, wasn't so different from the Weasel on a weeknight. He'd been so cocky about her interest in him, and less caring of what she'd think of his lack of funds. They were both students at the time, although he'd been well ahead of her, doing his master's in psychology, and none of their friends had a lot of disposable income—not even the ones from rich families like hers. School was expensive, and they all took it seriously.

Dan had never been driven by money. A good portion of his income went to various missions for children in third-world countries rather than fancy restaurants. He'd seen the real world on the company dime and had no interest in its whitewashed tourist destinations. That was what had really caught his attention about Alycia. She'd been unpretentious. Alive.

He was watching a hockey game when she arrived, but his team wasn't playing so he wasn't invested.

She looked so pretty as she pushed through the door that his heart skipped a beat, then took two or three extras in compensation. The weather had warmed since the last time he'd seen her. Rather than the royal-blue, bulky winter coat and white hat and scarf, she wore a body-hugging, wine-colored moto jacket that zipped up the side, thick black leggings, and short black leather boots with high, although sensible, heels. She must have walked.

He stood so she could see him, which she did almost at once.

Pretty was such an inadequate description for her. The hair, combined with the pale skin and electric-blue eyes, shot her looks off the charts. But she had more than looks going for her. She had a special charisma—a tangible aura that was undeniably hers. He could have his back to the door, and he'd still know who came through it.

He mumbled a greeting. She did the same.

Her dark red hair swept her shoulders as she shrugged out of the leather jacket to reveal a tight black turtleneck sweater underneath. He took her jacket and hung it on the hook beside their booth while trying to keep his eyes off her breasts.

The awkward part of this meeting now over, they chatted about the weather until the drink waitress came by. Alycia ordered one of the local craft beers from the specialty menu. He did the same.

"What do you recommend for food?" she inquired, flipping the menu over to see what the Weasel offered in that department.

"The Dragon's Breath Burger." One of those each and there'd be no question of any casual, good-night kisses between them. Or with anyone else. Not for weeks.

Those amazing eyes sparkled, letting him know she was in on the joke. "As tempting as that sounds, I try to be kind to my coworkers. They don't need to suffer tomorrow because of my dinner tonight."

"Since you put it that way...the Greasy Weasel Burger is the house favorite," he said. "People seem to like the sweet potato fries on the side, but I'm more of a traditionalist."

Alycia set the laminated menu down. "I'm in the mood to rebel. Sweet potato it is."

They placed their orders and sipped at their beers while they waited for food, and he forced himself to relax. He'd allow her to do the talking, to broach whatever topic she deemed a priority. All he had to do was to sit here and listen. That wasn't so hard.

For her part, all she had to do was not push him.

CHAPTER SIX

WHEN DAN INVITED HER out to dinner after rejecting her previous offer, Alycia hadn't been sure whether or not to accept. At the end of the day, curiosity won her over.

She got the impression he wanted to discuss more than work, and yet here he sat, waiting for her to get the conversational ball rolling. Whatever he wanted from her, he'd have to put in more effort than a recap of the weather. She heeded David's warning. She wasn't having dinner with an old acquaintance. She was dining with CSIS.

If only Dan didn't look so damned hot. The long-sleeved, stretchy nylon gray t-shirt defined every muscle in his arms and his chest. A black, ion-plated stainless steel diver's watch encircled one wrist. Jeans and black leather ankle boots completed the rugged ensemble. Cool hazel eyes that missed nothing, constantly roaming the room, were what put the lie to the ordinary image he tried to project. She'd once asked a violent repeat offender how he chose his targets. He looked for a lack of confidence and an opponent who didn't size him up. Given that criteria, Dan didn't need to worry about walking home alone late at night.

She was going to shake all of that cool.

Before she could come up with a question that might do the trick, a man materialized out of thin air at her elbow. Since she too was usually good at surveying a room, his sudden appearance came as a surprise. Her only defense for her inattention was that she'd been so distracted by Dan.

The newcomer reached past her to offer Dan his extended hand. The cuff of his sleeve rode up a few inches, far enough to expose a deep, ugly scar above his inner wrist. She knew a stab wound when she saw it.

"Hey," he said to Dan, but that he was curious about Alycia was plain. "I didn't expect to see you here tonight."

"Last-minute decision. I wasn't expecting you here tonight either." Dan introduced them. "Alycia, this is Bruno. He puts the weasel in greasy. He owns the place."

There was some kind of subtext going on. A code. She wondered what that was about.

Bruno was a little above average height with the build of a light heavyweight boxer. He had black curly hair and the face of a Greek statue. Another scar puckered the corner of his left eye. Whoever made that one hadn't been messing around.

"Interesting name for a pub," Alycia commented, shaking his hand. "Is there a story behind it?"

"Uh…" Bruno looked at Dan.

"Don't tell her," Dan advised him, one of his rare grins transforming his face. "She'll judge you."

"Forget I asked. I no longer want to know." Alycia's graduating class at the RCMP academy had been made up mostly of men. She worked in a male-dominated environment where maturity was a moving target. She smiled at Bruno, silently letting him know that she was fine with not being in on the joke. She could figure it out. "As long as the food's good, the name doesn't matter."

"The food is the best in the city."

"He says modestly," Dan interjected. "But it so happens he's right."

The men discussed hockey and the Senators' playoff chances before Bruno left to go check on his kitchen. Whatever he'd wanted to know when he came to their table, it seemed he'd found out.

Alycia's curiosity about their subtext wasn't satisfied yet. Bruno and Dan had some sort of professional connection. She had her purse on the bench seat beside her. She knocked it to the floor with her elbow and bent to retrieve it. As she did, she examined the underside of the table and found the audio scrambler.

"Is that really necessary?" she asked when she straightened.

Dan shrugged, not bothering to pretend he didn't know what she meant. "You never know."

"Are you taping our conversation too?"

"Like I'd say if I were."

Wow. She'd thought police officers were paranoid. "Empty your pockets."

He stuck his hands in his jeans. A pocket knife, a handful of quarters, and a crumpled parking stub landed on the table next to his wallet. "Satisfied?"

"Not yet." His jacket hung on the hook beside hers, near her head. She poked at it, feeling the lining and emptying those pockets too. She found an old grocery receipt and a packet of cough drops.

He held his arms out to the sides. "Want to pat me down while you're at it?"

"No." Not for a wire. If he had one with him he wouldn't go to that much effort to hide it. But the thought of running her hands over him for other reasons held an unsettling appeal. "There's something wrong with you," she added. "Who takes an audio scrambler to dinner?"

"It pays to be cautious. We're not on a date," he pointed out, as if she didn't already know.

Fine. They weren't on a date. He couldn't pretend this was entirely about business though. So what was his game?

Their food arrived. Alycia dragged a sweet potato fry through a small paper container of curried mayonnaise. The fries were hot and delicious. The thick burger on the focaccia bun, dripping with bacon and melted cheese, smelled equally good and she was hungry. She cut it in half with her knife and took a bite.

She swallowed the mouthful of burger, wiped her fingers on her paper napkin, and decided to get personal. She had questions, but she'd start with something easy. "You were studying psychology. What made you decide on espionage as a career path?"

"CSIS came to me with a tempting offer. I don't know how they got my name. My guess is a professor gave them a recommendation."

"What was the tempting offer?" What made it more appealing to him than her?

But that was the one question she wouldn't ask.

"Let's just say that CSIS knows how to get inside a candidate's head," Dan replied. "They did their homework."

"Any regrets?"

"About a million." He stuck a fry in his mouth and spoke around it. "No more than anyone else who settles into a long-term career. What about you? You aren't doing what you set out to do. What made you decide on the RCMP?"

"I realized I wasn't cut out for the life of an activist.

It's amazing how much a few days in a holding cell with no shower and a communal toilet changes your perspective about protesting."

His gaze made another sweep of the room before returning to her. There was no one sitting within earshot. Tuesday nights in the downtown business district weren't busy with locals, and the out-of-town businesspeople tended to stick to hotel bars.

"I'll be honest if you will," he said.

Honesty? She stared at her plate. The burger lost its appeal. Now she could say for certain that the conversation wasn't being recorded—assuming he meant what he said. But she'd give him the benefit of the doubt, since she had nothing to hide.

"Saving the whales became less important to me than salvaging humanity. Someone has to protect the people willing to do right."

She didn't have to mention any names. Dan would understand that she'd lost control of her life and her sense of right and wrong. The law provided guidelines she'd needed. She'd been well into her police training before she'd fully understood the law's complexities and that not everything was black and white. By then it was too late, and she was hooked.

Dan took another bite of his burger and chewed it as if he'd be writing a critique for a food column. She waited. She could be patient. He'd made the offer of honesty and he'd carry through, but in his own time and by his own definition.

"In order to go into war zones, I had to be free of commitment and one hundred percent focused on my training. I wanted excitement enough to agree." He looked at the untouched half of her burger. "You going to eat that?"

She pushed her plate across the table to him. He took the burger and added it to his.

"That's it? You chose to go into war zones because you wanted excitement?" she asked, incredulous. He said it the same way he might declare he preferred ketchup to mustard. "Why not take up skydiving?"

"I've done that too."

"Who *are* you?" she demanded, only half-kidding. "It's like I've never met you before." The Dan she'd known had been quiet. Focused. Studious and steady. She'd been the life of the party whereas he'd preferred to sit back and watch. They'd complemented each other.

Or so she'd thought.

"I was a twenty-six-year-old grad student," he reminded her. "I hadn't found myself. I watched you take on so many causes with an enthusiasm I could never figure out. It's not that I didn't believe in what you were doing, but I bypassed all that enthusiasm and went straight to where I believed I could do the most good. I found the path that worked for me."

The path that worked for him... She pondered that for a long moment. For years, she'd been caught up in all the ways Dan had failed her. Never once had she considered the possibility that she might have failed him instead. She wished she could turn back the clock. She'd make so many changes. She'd known what she wanted. Somehow she'd missed this side of him.

"I'm so sorry," she said.

He tilted his head, his brows pinching his forehead. "For what?"

"For not being supportive when you told me about joining CSIS. I should have wished you well and encouraged you. Instead, I made it all about me."

His forehead smoothed. His hazel eyes lost their chill.

"You were twenty-one. You hadn't found yourself either. I don't think either one of us handled it as well as we could have. We were so different, but also too much alike."

"Alike?" If they were, she couldn't see it. "In what way?"

"We were both all or nothing."

She munched another one of her fries. "You're right. If you hadn't broken up with me, I would have told you to choose. You'd have chosen CSIS and the end result would have been the same. Only the fight would have been different."

"Do you think now we can move forward?" Dan asked.

She hoped so. He'd been her first love. Maybe they couldn't go back, but she was so glad he was alive and they'd had this talk. Now she could remember their days together not with sadness or anger, but as a period of mutual growth. They'd been happy, but love could carry a couple only so far, and he'd been smart enough to figure that out. He was trying to tell her that he was no longer interested in her. He'd chosen his career over her and his mind hadn't changed in that regard.

Except she didn't believe him. He hadn't ended that kiss at his front door. And his continued insistence that they look forward suggested he was the one who'd never gotten over the past, which was something else that didn't make sense. He'd been the one to walk away from her.

Unless his reluctance to get too close to her had something to do with what happened to Terry—something Dan hadn't told her—and that, she refused to believe. No one was that good a liar.

"Yes, we can move forward." She gave him her hand

and they shook across the table. Their palms fit well together. His grip was solid and warm. "Hi. I'm Alycia Evers. I believe we have a case to work on together."

By the time they finished their dinner and conversation, which had moved on to business, hours had passed and it was late.

Dan insisted on walking Alycia back to her condo because she refused to tie up a cab for such a short distance, even though the pub sat at the far end of a poorly lit side street, foot traffic was spare at this hour on a weeknight, and the city's crime stats weren't at zero. They'd run out of work to discuss and settled on silence, each lost in their own thoughts.

Dan's were chaotic. He hadn't been one hundred percent honest, omitting a small detail when giving his reason for breaking up with her. He'd agreed to concentrate on his CSIS training without any distractions in those early days, true, but he'd never planned on spending years in unsettled locations. Maybe one year, at the most two. In his heart he'd believed that when he was ready she'd be waiting for him.

She hadn't waited. And he had no one to blame for that but himself.

On a street corner, in the shadows, a lonely figure wrapped in blankets huddled on the cold sidewalk, slumped against the side of a building, out of the wind. The temperature had dropped considerably throughout the evening.

Beside Dan, Alycia's steps slowed. If she'd been alone she would likely have crossed the street, a wise move for a woman, but that wasn't Dan's way. He didn't alter his path, forging ahead and dragging her with him.

A head emerged from the blankets as they approached. "Got any spare change?" a weary voice asked. The tone indicated low expectations.

A teenager. Male. Between the ages of sixteen and eighteen, kids like this slid through the cracks of the system—too old for protective services but too young to collect welfare. Many left home because home was worse than the streets.

Dan dug out his wallet and extracted a five-dollar bill before passing it over. The bill disappeared into the folds of the blanket. The teen muttered a few words of thanks.

Alycia hunkered down on her heels. "It's cold out," she said to the boy. "I can call someone to pick you up and take you to the Ottawa Mission for the night."

"No. I'll get a coffee. That's all I need."

Dan hustled Alycia off before she could call the city police and have the kid picked up for vagrancy—an archaic law the authorities used not to lay charges against them, but as an excuse to get kids like this into a shelter.

When they were out of earshot, she gave him a scolding. "You shouldn't have given him money. It will get him into a coffee shop so he can use the facilities, but it will also keep him on the street for a few more days. He won't look for the help he needs. You would have been better off letting me call the police and giving your money to the Mission."

"Spoken like a police officer. You're going to call them anyway. But he needed a coffee right now, and maybe to believe a little in the kindness of other human beings."

She cocked her head to one side. "How do you know he'll spend the money on coffee?"

"How do you know he won't?" Dan shot back.

"There's not much else you can do with five bucks. Besides, the moment I handed the money over, I gave up any right to tell him what to do with it."

Alycia stopped walking. They'd reached her condo. She had her hands in her jacket pockets. Her purse was tucked beneath one arm, the shoulder strap securely crossing her body.

"As an FYI, Captain Humanity, I gave that same kid twenty dollars on my way to meet you. Since he doesn't appear to be high, I'll leave him alone and see if he's still there in the morning. If he is, that's when I'll start asking questions."

This was an unexpected turn of events, and Dan had no idea what to say. "So why am I getting a lecture?"

"Because I know what my motives were for giving him money. I've worked with street kids, and yes, I know a shelter's not always the answer either. I was curious about your reasons." Her eyes searched his face. "Does your boss know you've gotten soft?"

"Bite your tongue. Maybe you've become a cynical hard-ass, Officer Evers. Ever think of that?"

But Dan had to smile. He liked the woman she'd developed into. She'd come out the other end of a senseless tragedy a lot stronger than he'd given her credit for. Damaged, perhaps. But weren't they all in some way?

The wind swirling around the side of her building caught a potato chip bag in its updraft. The bag touched the ground for a second, skittered a few feet like a pebble skipped across water, then became airborne. A breath of snow lingered in escaped pockets of air that bit at his cheeks, and he rolled up his jacket collar. Winter wasn't quite over.

"Would you like to come up and get warm?" Alycia asked.

He had no trouble reading the real question she posed. She was curious as to how deep the attraction between them still ran, and he wasn't ready to be alone with her again to find out. It didn't take his master's degree in psychology to know he suffered survivor's guilt over a decision he'd made a long time ago, even if it had been the right one to make. She'd become a reward he didn't believe he was entitled to. He didn't know how to get past that sensation. "Another time, maybe."

They looked at each other. One of them had to say good night first.

"This is ridiculous." She laughed a little, shaking her head. "We're adults. We've known each other a long time. We should be able to treat each other as more than business acquaintances without it being weird." She threw her arms around his neck and gave him a kiss on the cheek. "Good night, Dan. Thank you for dinner and walking me home."

She didn't, however, let go.

That was when things did get weird.

He caught the scent of her skin—the combination of fresh, outdoor air and a subtle perfume—then felt the light brush of the top of her head against the underside of his chin. The attraction was still there between them. And the heat. Underneath the layer of professional ice, she had the same fire he'd never been able to resist. He used to love staying up the whole night making love to her, despite having papers to write and early morning tutorials to attend.

He spread his palms against the small of her back, the smooth leather of her jacket cold to the touch, and drew her against him. A stray flake of snow had gotten tangled in one of her long lashes, fluttering like a leaf on a breeze. He bent his head, his lips seeking hers.

Her mouth was soft, her lips slightly parted. He slid his tongue between them. She tasted of the peppermint she'd picked up at the counter by the pub door on their way out. He could hear his heart beating, the thud of it loud in his ears.

A horn blared. "Get a room!" someone shouted from a passing car.

Dan broke off the kiss. He had one hand on her ass and the other under her jacket, with one of his knees pressed between her thighs. They were standing on the sidewalk in front of her building, where any of her neighbors might see them, as tightly together as two fully clothed people could be.

"Come upstairs with me," she whispered, her hands clasped behind his neck and her eyes searching his face.

He pressed his forehead against hers and closed his eyes. "I can't do this."

She pulled back, putting a few feet of space between them, darting a bold, pointed glance at his crotch. Her breath puffed like steam in the cold air as she dared to tease him, something few people did. He wasn't known for a great sense of humor. "Don't tell me—you prefer to work alone."

"No." He had an aching erection to prove that he didn't, and since it was doubtful she'd missed it, she deserved a plausible explanation for the mixed signals he was sending. He jammed his hands in his pockets. "We're working together. I mean on the investigation," he added, and felt his face turning red.

"You've got to be kidding me. No one's that dedicated to a career. Since we're on the same side and work in different departments, I don't think it matters as long as we aren't chasing each other naked around anyone's office." She crossed her arms and lifted her chin in a direct challenge. "Don't make up lame excuses. If you don't want me, come right out and say so. Although for the record, I'm not going to believe you."

She had good reason not to. He'd been as deep into that kiss as she was.

His fists tightened and he felt torn in ways that were impossible to explain. As much as he wanted to, he couldn't get past all the memories and guilt.

"I can see you're overthinking this." She slid her hand into his jacket pocket and pried his fist open, linking her fingers with his. "Let me make it easier for you. This is an invitation to come back to my place and see where the rest of the evening takes us. I can scrounge up a spare toothbrush, but I'm not clearing out closet space so you can move in."

The logical part of his brain told him to relax. She was right, and he was getting ahead of himself. The other part of his brain, however—the one that knew him the best— said she was pushing all the right buttons. It shouted *Danger*.

And Dan had always been a huge sucker for that.

Her fingers tightened as if she sensed weakness. She liberated their joined hands from his pocket. "Since you can't make up your mind, let me make it up for you. You told me that when you were twenty-six you wanted excitement. When did you lose your sense of adventure? When did you become such an old man?"

"Right about the same time other people's lives began to depend on me and the decisions I make. I have a whole team that loves the curmudgeon I've turned into."

She laughed at him, her eyes dancing. The cold had reddened her cheeks and the tip of her nose. "That's work. We're talking play. Two separate things."

It was her laughter that got him. He liked it so much

better than sadness and tears. It said she wasn't taking this anywhere near as seriously as he was and any hang-ups were his. She was thirty-two years old—with a birthday coming up soon—and knew what she was doing.

"My arthritic hip might prove to be a big disappointment," he said, giving in.

She tugged on his hand. "I'll keep my expectations low and the ibuprofen handy."

He followed her inside, testosterone reassuring his conscience that this was about sex between two consenting adults, nothing more. There'd be no teary meltdowns. No smell of roses.

But she could keep her spare toothbrush. He wouldn't be spending the night.

CHAPTER SEVEN

THEY BARELY MADE IT through the door of her condo before she was caught up in Dan's arms, his lips sliding hungrily over hers. Her skin tingled, excitement threading its way through her body and melting her bones.

The way he kissed her removed any lingering doubts. He was as into her as she was him. Whatever his reluctance—whatever was going on in his head—she'd let him work it out in his own way. Tonight was about play, just as she'd told him. She wasn't demanding any commitments. She no longer believed he was capable of making them, anyway. He probably never had been, and she'd been too in love and naïve to figure it out. She wouldn't be making that mistake with him again.

But they'd been aware of each other all evening—in fact, since that morning in John Carmichael's office—and the sex had always been good. As long as they both knew where things stood, they'd be fine.

He broke the kiss first, his breathing unsteady. "There are some safe sex issues we should discuss."

"I haven't had sex in three years, but I have myself tested regularly." She shed her coat and boots as she spoke, seeing no need to mention the two years after Terry's

death, when she'd gone through a series of brief affairs—
many of them one-time hook-ups with other police
officers—because she'd been lonely but uninterested in
commitment. Once she'd gotten her head straightened out
and acknowledged that sex for the sake of it wasn't a smart
alternative, she'd chosen her partners with a great deal
more care. Whenever things got too serious, however, the
panic attacks reemerged and she ended things.

"Three *years*? Six months for me. Maybe seven or
eight. I can't really remember," he confessed.

She was too pleased by that revelation, considering
they were keeping things light. "That good, was it?"

"It was great," he assured her. "Have no fears about
that. But we have a different problem. I don't have any
condoms on me."

"I have plenty, although the box might be dusty."

He blinked as if taken aback. "Plenty, huh?" He
collected himself while hanging his coat on a hook. "Any
handcuffs to go with them?"

Alycia hooked a finger on one of the belt loops on his
jeans, her knuckle grazing the solid abdominal muscle
beneath, and led him to the bedroom as she spoke. "Not
anymore. Now that I'm an investigator, I don't get to
make many arrests. I had to turn them in—along with my
gun."

"Disappointing. But I can work with limitations. A
couple of scarves will do the trick."

This was a side of him that she'd never known, and
yes, she found it intriguing. "Hold on a second. Who are
we talking about tying up?"

He dug in his heels at the bedroom door, jerking them
both to a halt. He caught her arm, pulling her against him.
He tipped his head to the side as he studied her face. "I
thought you wanted to play."

She did, but saw no reason to tell him how much. It might scare him off. "That depends. Exactly what kind of games are you into these days?"

Light fingers burrowed under her hair, cupping the back of her neck. A thumb rolled across her bottom lip. "How far are you willing to go to find out? How much control are you willing to give me?"

He was testing her. He used to call her Miss Bossy Pants for a reason. They'd had a great sex life, but they'd both been inexperienced and she'd called all the shots. He was letting her know that tonight things were going to be different.

She looked forward to it. "Your wish is my command—on the condition that whatever you do to me, I get to do to you."

A slow smile spread across his face, flowing upward from his lips to his eyes. Meanwhile, for her, heat shot in an entirely different direction. He could have her right here, up against the door frame, if he gave the word. She wanted him *now*.

"Some of it might be anatomically impossible because we're working with different plumbing," he said, "but I get your point. You've got a deal."

She eased her palm under his shirt and into the front of his jeans, crossing the flat plane of his stomach until her fingers encountered coarse, tight curls and a promising ridge of hot flesh. He'd gone commando.

She pressed her breasts against him, rubbing her thigh against the bulge of his erection for added effect. "My safe word is Sally."

That threw him again, but just for a second. He ran his hand down her hip, then gave one of her butt cheeks a light, playful slap before spinning her around and sending her into the bedroom ahead of him. "Be a good girl and go get me those scarves. While you're at it, you might as well bring the whole box of condoms."

"What about lubricant?"

"I've never had a woman need it yet." His confident grin held a promise that had her panties damp with anticipation, which suggested his record would stand undefeated, but she wasn't going down without a fight.

"Oh, it's not for me. It's for when my turn comes." She tossed that over her shoulder, leaving him with something to think about as she opened the walk-in closet door.

She got the scarves—the blue was her favorite—and then found the box of condoms in the back of a cupboard in her bedroom en suite. When she reemerged, Dan was stretched out fully clothed on her bed, watching her, no doubt searching for signs she was bluffing about agreeing to bondage. The room was semi-dark, lit by the city outside of the window. She debated drawing the curtains, but anyone looking in would see very little. Dan was the one she didn't want missing the show. He was asking for this.

They were about to find out who was bluffing. She had the condoms in one hand and the scarves in the other. She held them up. "Where would you like them?"

He pointed to the table beside her bed. "Set them right here. We'll get to them in good time."

She put the box down and then waited for further instructions, determined to do as she was told but to put her own spin on things while she was at it. He wanted to be in charge? Then let him take charge.

She dared him.

He folded his hands behind his head. "Take off your sweater."

She peeled it over her head, turning it inside out before letting it fall to the floor from the tips of her fingers.

Underneath, she wore a navy push-up bra. She could tell by the way his eyes darkened that he liked what he saw.

"Now the pants."

She took her time stripping the leggings, never taking her gaze off his hungry expression. His attention was all on her body, which suited her fine. She had nothing to hide and very few inhibitions. The bikini panties matched her bra—two small, transparent triangles of lace held together by thin strips of navy elastic.

"God, you're beautiful, Allie."

He'd said the same words to her before. More than once. But she forced her thoughts not to go there. Those days were gone, and to be truthful, she was no longer sorry about it. She couldn't wait to find out what secrets this new Dan was hiding.

She waited for his next set of instructions, which weren't long in coming.

"Lose the bra first."

She reached behind her and unhooked the clasp, working the straps down her arms with her thumbs and allowing her breasts to fall free. The bra joined the clothes she'd already discarded.

His breath rasped. "Touch them for me. Show me what you like."

He'd promised to allow her to do to him whatever he did to her, so she'd do whatever he asked. She cupped her breasts in her palms and ran her thumbs over her nipples, lowering her eyes and arching her back. "Like this?" She exhaled. Excitement sent a wave of fire to the swollen juncture between her thighs.

"Exactly like that." He sounded strangled. "But close your eyes and imagine it's me touching you. Show me what I do to you. How do I make you feel?"

She did as he said, unprepared for her physical reaction

once her eyes were shut and she was alone with her imagination. The thought of him watching her—of touching herself the way she'd like him to do—was unbelievably exciting. He'd been right about not needing lubrication. He hadn't done anything himself yet, and already, her panties were soaked.

"Get rid of the panties."

He had to be reading her mind. Completely naked now, and enjoying the performance far more than she'd expected, she slid a hand down her belly to tangle in the knot of tight, dark-red curls. "Do you want me to touch myself...here?"

He was sitting upright by now. His erection strained at his zipper. "I think I can manage the rest on my own. Come here."

She wedged her legs between his thighs, the denim grazing her skin. He took her hips in his hands and leaned forward to press a kiss to her bare stomach. She sucked in a breath. One of his palms slid to her naked buttocks, the other eased between her legs. He stroked the tip of a finger along her damp folds, then slowly, gently, eased it inside her. A small gasp of pleasure escaped her. The reality was far better than any thought of him touching her would ever be. She thrust her pelvis against his hand, urging him deeper. Harder. She scarcely registered the crooning sounds of encouragement he gave her. "Come for me, Allie. I've got you. Let it go."

She gripped his shoulders and exploded. Her legs trembled as she collapsed in his arms, gasping for air while she regained her sanity. He'd learned a few things over the years. In fact, he'd mastered them.

He held her, his face pressed into her hair with her cheek against his chest. She was naked. He was still fully clothed.

"It's my turn," she said. She'd learned a few things too, and wanted to make sure he knew it.

His laugh shook through his chest. "I don't think so. We're just getting started."

Dan didn't doubt for a second that there would be payback for issuing commands to her, or that it would be worth it.

He'd read the promise of retribution in Alycia's eyes when he'd asked her to touch herself. He'd also taken note of the interest and excitement they held, and continued to hold. He hadn't been at all prepared for how willing she was or how hot he found it. Thank God he'd left his clothes on or the night would be over.

But he wouldn't have them on for much longer. He reached for the two scarves Alycia had left by the bed. Good thing they were long. The bed was a queen with posts on either side of the headboard.

"Lie on your stomach," he said. He tied the scarves to her wrists and their ends to the posts. All of that smooth, creamy-white skin... He'd dreamed of it so many times. Her legs were well-muscled, her glutes clearly defined. She worked out, and it showed. He tracked a light finger down the length of her spine, then tapped at the base where the cleft of her buttocks began. "Lift your hips."

He slid a pillow under her stomach. She had her face turned to one side with her cheek pressed into the mattress, watching him with curious, heavy-lidded eyes that made it impossible for him to concentrate on what he was doing to her. He couldn't have that. He planned on giving her as much pleasure first as he could. He wanted her begging for more, not plotting revenge.

"I'm going to have to blindfold you, too." He found another scarf in her closet, a pink one this time, and tied it snugly in place.

"Am I allowed to talk while you work?" Her throaty sigh almost had him unloading right there.

"As long as the sentence contains 'give me' and 'more.' And sweetheart, this isn't work. Not by a long shot," he added. "If you don't remember the difference, you've been doing it wrong."

Once he had her arranged how he wanted and made sure she was comfortable, he took off his clothes and rejoined her on the bed. The pale light gave him a great view of her naked body, hips high, her thighs spread and ready for him. With her blindfolded, he could look all he liked without any distractions. The blindfold served a dual purpose, however. He had a few scars he wasn't ready to explain. That would be a definite mood killer. He straddled her legs, his hard, heavy erection pressing against soft feminine flesh. He had his hands on her ass and he caressed her round cheeks with his thumbs. She was already damp from coming for him once. She'd come at least once more before he'd allow himself inside her.

And then he'd make damn sure she came a third time.

He leaned forward and placed the tip of his tongue to her folds, licking upward until he found the small nib he was seeking. When he had it, he sucked. She cried out, her hips jerking as she moaned his name and something inarticulate, her pleasure unmistakable. But she was holding back, her hands curled in fists as she tried to restrain a second orgasm, no doubt waiting for him.

There'd be plenty of time for that. He ran his palms up her sides, his hands spanning her narrow waist as he held her hips still. He thrust his tongue deep inside her, stroking in and out, enjoying her sweet, salty taste.

"Stop, Dan!" she gasped, her voice hoarse with unfulfilled desire as she tugged against the restraints. "I can't take it. I'm going to come and I want you inside me. I want to *touch* you and make you come too."

He paused. She liked what he was doing. She liked it a lot. But he had to be sure. "Stop, stop? Or 'Don't stop doing what you're doing to me, Dan?'"

"Don't stop," she bit out without the slightest hesitation, wriggling her hips in impatience. "You're on your own."

"Then what did I tell you?" he demanded, despite an aching need to replace his tongue with a different instrument. "The words are 'give me' and 'more.'"

He dipped his tongue in again, nipping her delicate flesh gently with his teeth. He could feel the small interior muscles begin to tighten and clench, building to the orgasm she couldn't possibly contain. It rocked through her, her slight frame arching into a bow as she lifted her head off the bed. Once the orgasm passed, several long seconds later, she collapsed in a trembling mass.

"I had no idea Canadian spies were allowed to torture their prisoners," she panted. "What did they teach you in spy school?"

Dan, his erection raging for attention by now, was lost in his own inarticulate haze of desire. He could smell her release. Taste it on his lips and his tongue. Her skin felt so perfect under his hands. But he could wait for her to be ready for him again. While he'd never expected any of this to happen, he'd had a long time to think about it.

He pressed a string of light kisses up her back before stretching out to sprawl on the bed beside her. He draped an arm over her ribs and nuzzled the side of her throat, his erection pressing between them. He waited patiently while her breathing slowly steadied and his appetite for her receded to a bearable level.

"*Now* is it my turn?" she whispered—amusement mixed with frustration. She had her face nestled into his shoulder, but she couldn't see anything because of the blindfold.

"You're terrible at taking direction," he chided her. "How did you ever make it through police training?" He ran his tongue over the rim of her ear and she shivered against him. "What words are you supposed to be using?"

Her laugh turned into a rueful sigh that tickled his flesh. "I'm not really sure you can give me more than you just did."

"Challenge accepted. I'll bet I can."

He cupped her face in his hands and kissed her, brushing his lips back and forth over hers, then teasing hers apart with his tongue.

His patience had been stretched to its limits. He knelt over her again, tightening the blindfold and checking the bindings on her wrists to make sure they were loose but secure. He considered releasing her, or at least turning her to her back so she could enjoy the full frontal experience, but decided against it. Despite her half-hearted protests, she liked what he was doing already, so he saw no need to go switching things up. Not yet.

He rested one palm on her lower back and took his erection in hand, sliding its rounded tip between her raised buttocks—not for penetration, but to rub up and down against her so he could gauge her readiness for him. The pale light from the uncovered window splashed across the bed, illuminating the expression of intense concentration on her face. Her arms jerked, her hands curling into fists before she began flexing her fingers.

He fumbled for the box of condoms. They were ribbed, which piqued his interest. Out of the pack of twenty-four a handful were missing. He grabbed one packet and tore it open with his teeth, then rolled the condom into place.

He positioned his sheathed erection at the soft, swollen flesh of her entry. He slid the head inside her, then withdrew. Slowly.

"Give me more!" she demanded, her hips thrusting upward.

"Hang on, Bossy Pants. What kind of man would I be if I rushed things?" He pressed her into the mattress with his splayed palm, holding her steady. Again he inched inside her, a little farther this time, before withdrawing. He repeated the action over and over until his whole shaft was buried, his sac was slapping its heavy weight against her, and she was rocking in enthusiastic rhythm. His hands and knees were shaking by now, the sensations too varied and wild to describe. She was so hot and tight. The sounds of encouragement she made, her cries of pleasure alternating with pleas for more, drove him on. He was so close, but he wanted her with him.

When the first spasms of her third orgasm made her clench around him, pulsing and massaging the rigid length of his shaft, his body decided he'd held back long enough. He came on such a wave of intensity that for a moment, his vision blurred. That loud groan of satisfaction was probably his.

He stayed on his knees, his hands on the swell of her hips, his fingers lightly stroking her skin. *What are you doing here, Hanson?* He would have loved to remain where he was, deep inside her, enjoying the loss of every last bit of control he possessed, but he wasn't that irresponsible. They weren't using foolproof protection, and he wasn't going to screw up her life a third time. He withdrew, then got out of bed to dispose of the used condom in Alycia's en suite.

When he returned, he untied her hands and removed the blindfold. She rolled to her back. Wide, long-lashed blue eyes—so dark they appeared solid black in the dim light—stared up at him. A slight frown puckered her lips in a way that had him longing to kiss her again, and wondering if a fourth orgasm would be expecting too much.

"Who *are* you?" she asked. "Have we ever met?"

The question was valid, sincere, and not without justification. He had no ready answer. He'd never done anything remotely like this with her—or any woman for that matter. Domination—even on the mild end of the spectrum—had never appealed to him. If he were to put his college degree to good use and examine his actions, he might conclude that he hadn't wanted tonight to resemble anything close to what they'd once had between them. He hadn't expected her to participate with such overwhelming enthusiasm.

The missing condoms crossed his mind, not out of jealousy or judgment—he had no grounds for either—but curiosity. Enough had been used to indicate that three years ago, her sex life had been healthy. And the fact that she'd relied on condoms suggested to him that while it might have been healthy, it hadn't been conducted with anyone serious. When they were together she'd taken a birth control pill.

As for why she'd bought ribbed... Someone hadn't been living up to expectations, and it sure as hell wasn't him. He did things right.

"There you go, overthinking. Quit being so serious, Dan. It was a joke." She hooked the back of his thigh with her foot and pulled him onto the bed. "This is playtime, remember?" She shifted to her side and propped her head on her hand, watching his face. "Or is that arthritic hip acting up?"

"The hip is just fine."

He toyed with a lock of her hair, rubbing it between his fingers. He wanted her desperately. And not just for sex. She was all the things he'd never be—smart, uninhibited, willing to share whatever she was feeling at any given moment. His world was full of shadows. She was light.

Having her didn't mean happiness was guaranteed. He didn't know how to reconcile the past with the present— and if he couldn't get over his guilt surrounding Terry's death, she'd serve as a constant reminder. He'd end up making her miserable too, and that was the last thing he'd ever want. She'd rebuilt her life, and it was a good one. She seemed content.

He wasn't and never would be. Pieces of him were missing. Being in the same city with her, now that he knew she was here, would be too much for his mental wellbeing once playtime was over. When her investigation was finished, and his part in it complete, he was asking John for a transfer. He'd go back into fieldwork and take a team on the road if he had to. An office was stifling, the rules too restrictive, and he hated enforcing them with intelligence officers whom he trusted to use their own judgment.

He glanced at the digital clock on the nightstand, its red numbers gleaming. The three flipped over to a four. "It's going to be morning soon. We both have to work."

She didn't suggest he spend what remained of the night in her bed as he was half-afraid she might. He didn't know what to make of that. He swung his legs out of bed and scooped up his clothes. The harsh rasp of the zipper's slider against metal teeth filled the room as he fastened the fly of his jeans by the faint light from the window. She watched him, her sleepy eyes scanning his body in a satisfied way. She stretched and yawned, at ease with her own nakedness, and he had to admit, he liked what he saw too. He'd explored pretty much every inch of it tonight.

By now he'd moved across the room to the door and had one foot in the hall. Escape was a footfall away. He brought the other foot down an instant too late.

"You owe me, Dan," she called after him. "I intend to collect. Don't you dare think I'll forget."

He didn't stop or make a response, because he wasn't capable of it, but as he waited for the elevator in the silent hallway outside of her condo, he did accept the inevitable. He'd done everything he could to show her he wasn't the man she remembered. His problem was that she wasn't the woman he'd left behind either.

He wanted her. Even more than before.

And, at least until they were no longer working together, she could be his.

CHAPTER EIGHT

SEVEN HOURS LATER, ALYCIA'S body continued to thrum with a physical satisfaction she hadn't experienced in a very long time. But Dan had been trying to prove something last night, and she couldn't quite figure out what.

She was tired and distracted, so it took a second for her brain to home in on what David was telling her on the other end of the phone. *The Prime Minister's Office isn't on board.*

The special prosecutor's words burned through her afterglow. Alycia clutched the telephone receiver. "What reason did they give?"

"The PMO doesn't want to charge a sitting minister," David explained. "They're worried about public perception at home and abroad. Global Affairs stepped in and concurred with the PMO because of the potential for international conflict—just as I warned you they would. They're insisting on a meeting with you, me, and Dan Hanson. I spoke to one of my contacts in the PMO privately to see if I could pinpoint their concerns. She said a lot of the evidence CSIS gave you indicates several foreign allies were willing participants in the purchase of stolen Canadian military goods. The countries that weren't aware of what was going on inside their borders had their trade treaties compromised by Canadian ex-pats. And having those ex-pats connected to a sitting member of parliament? The PMO doesn't want to find itself in a position where the prime minister is forced to explain that."

This wasn't news Alycia wanted to hear, but it wasn't unexpected either, so she'd already put some thought into how to circumvent any possible objections the PMO might raise.

"How about if we amend the charges and come up with something that keeps everything within Canadian borders? Or—better yet—flips any international connections to non-government players a step removed from the defense minister?"

"You mean like Mike Freeland, the lawyer?" David asked, quickly grasping her line of thinking. "The recording your CSIS friend claims they have in their possession supposedly implicates Freeland in the sale of goods to the Ukraine, so it might be enough—as long as it comes from a reputable source. And as long as CSIS remains committed to seeing this through, even if we take the minister out of the equation," he added, his warning clear.

And...they were back to the original problem. David had a thing about CSIS's motives and dubious sources of intelligence. Dan, however, was one of the good guys. A man didn't change at his core, and Alycia had complete confidence in his integrity. His openness?

Not so much.

"There's little point in having a spy agency if we can't trust them at all." She drummed her fingers on her desk. "Leave it with me, and I'll see what information I can come up with if I have to switch the focus of the investigation over to Freeland."

This was a minor setback. She'd suffered worse. She'd find a way to bring it back to the defense minister, even if it meant using a circuitous route. They could always leak information to the press and let them confirm it, as David had already suggested.

But that would take time. Possibly years.

She yawned as she hung up the phone. It was only eleven thirty in the morning. Between worry over David's phone call, lack of sleep, and emotions that spanned an entire spectrum, she'd have a hard time keeping her brain engaged in her work for another five or six hours. This might be a good day to go through files and maybe see if her aunt was free for that lunch they kept promising each other.

She could use some advice.

She fired off a quick text message. Her aunt responded a few minutes later, naming a restaurant at a midpoint between them.

Alycia got there ten minutes late thanks to a lack of parking, so the lunch business was already booming, but Meredith had managed to snag them a table.

"Since we're meeting in public, not my office, I'm going to assume you have a personal matter you wish to discuss," her aunt said once Alycia was seated and they'd both ordered the special. She was not a woman to waste valuable time.

"Can't I have lunch with my favorite aunt without there being any problem?"

"Of course you can, darling." Her aunt's tone suggested *when pigs fly, but sure, I'll play along.*

"Fine," Alycia said. "I want your opinion about something."

"Tell Auntie Meredith all about it."

Alycia had gone to her aunt numerous times over the years. Meredith had been there for her throughout high school dramas and her breakup with Dan. When Terry was murdered, she'd done her best to get the details, protect Alycia from the worst of them, and make sure Alycia got out of bed every morning during the dark weeks that followed. There wasn't much about Alycia's personal life that Meredith didn't know.

Discussing her sex life with her aunt, however, was one step too far. Alycia was more interested in getting her take on what was behind Dan's hot-and-cold behavior. She might trust his personal integrity, but that was where her faith in him ended. He hadn't encouraged any intimacy from her at all, and she hadn't asked for it in return, but this wasn't the man she remembered. He'd been intent on satisfying her last night, yes—and lord, how he'd succeeded—yet when it came to his own needs he'd been hands-off. She refused to accept that the warm man who'd once loved spending hours in bed now cut and ran once the act was complete. Emotionally, there was something dead inside him, and if she was ever to let go of him and their past, she had to know why. Otherwise, she'd always wonder.

"Do you remember the man I dated in university?" she asked. "The one who broke up with me without any explanation?" That wasn't the whole truth, but it was the story she'd given her family. They didn't know he'd gone to work for CSIS—or that he'd been Terry's best friend.

"How could I forget? You cried for weeks over him."

"I was prone to melodrama," Alycia admitted. If only she'd known the universe had much, much worse in store for her.

Meredith patted her hand. "You were young and had your first real broken heart. You were allowed to be a little dramatic. I'm going to assume the reason you're bringing him up now is because he's come back into your life?" The family hadn't encouraged Alycia to date after Terry, but they'd never given up hope.

"Through work."

Alycia didn't have to say more than that. Her aunt knew what departments were involved in the investigation and Alycia could see her connecting the dots in her head. She hadn't gotten to her high level by being slow.

Meredith deliberately withdrew her hand from Alycia's, concern and disapproval now on open display. She switched from her role as loving aunt to Director of Special Prosecutions and personal mentor. "I see. If you want my advice, it's to stay far, far away." She spoke in a tone barely audible across the table for two. "He could ruin your career. There'd be such a conflict of interest if he had access to your resources and files. You could never trust him and right now you can't afford to take those kinds of risks."

The professional risk associated with Dan being CSIS had seemed so remote. They were on the same team, and she'd been more intent on protecting her heart—which began to beat a bit faster. Meredith was right. They might be on the same team, but only for this one particular investigation.

"He doesn't have access to anything work-related."

"No?" Meredith's eyebrows rode up her forehead. "Do you ever take work home? Has he been in your condo?" When Alycia didn't deny either she leaned forward, her palms on the table, driving her point deeper. "Do you understand how good these people are at collecting information? Do you realize they swap it like business cards? They take the phrase 'the ends justify the means' to a whole different level."

Was that why he was holding back on her? He planned to use her and her position and didn't want to become too emotionally involved?

Alycia didn't believe that. She'd pursued him since they'd reconnected, not the other way around. He'd wanted nothing to do with her. Or was she being naïve where he was concerned? Had he known her well enough to know she couldn't leave him alone? That she required closure between them? Had he seen an opportunity and run with it?

What would happen if he had to pursue her instead?

Now that doubts had been raised—or to be honest, confirmed—they refused to be silenced. Her head ached as lack of sleep and the roller coaster ride she'd been on finally hit her. The familiar sensation of an encroaching panic attack crawled up her arms and into her chest, where it threatened to settle. She took a deep breath and counted to ten, then let it go.

The dizziness passed. She'd come here for her aunt's opinion, and she'd gotten it. If she didn't like what she heard, that was on her.

"How serious is this relationship?" Meredith was asking.

"Not at all," Alycia replied, which was the truth. The sex had been fantastic. Any rekindled connection between them? Any tenderness or affection?

Nonexistent.

"Stay away from him," her aunt repeated. She signaled to the waiter for the check and reached for her purse. "I mean it." Her gaze softened, her next words proving she hadn't missed Alycia's panicked reaction. "And not just for the sake of your career. He's from a point in your past that holds a lot of bad memories. Do you really want to go there again?"

No.

That left her with one of two choices. She could focus on the present and the fantastic sex, but if she did, she'd be flirting with danger. While she wasn't interested in romance and felt confident he wasn't either, they were only human and feelings could change.

Her second option was to play it safe and end things right now.

Dan sipped at his beer, making it last. It was frothy and cold, the tall glass sweating in the warm room. Four days and counting, and Alycia hadn't yet called in his debt. What was the holdup?

She had, however, called to tell him that the PMO was reluctant to move forward with charges, keeping the conversation crisp and professional. She wanted a transcript of the wiretap his intelligence officer, Lies Wiersma, had recorded in the Netherlands. She didn't say why.

And he hadn't agreed to give it to her, which was the reason he and John Carmichael were sitting in the Greasy Weasel late on Friday afternoon, having a beer at the end of a long week. CSIS didn't want to hand the transcript over too early. Once the information was out, Bernard Vanderloord would know exactly where it came from and Dan's intelligence officer would be compromised. So would Canada's defense trade commissioner to the Netherlands, who'd used his position and played a subordinate role.

Taking Bernard Vanderloord out of the equation would create a problem. Not for Dan. As far as he was concerned, Vanderloord would get what he deserved—and what the crime boss had given to others without thinking twice. The problem was that Vanderloord sat at the hub of the supply chain that they were pursuing. With him gone, the supply chain would briefly crumble, then reassemble with someone else at its core. And CSIS would be back to chasing raindrops.

A second problem—and this one was Dan's—was that Alycia would never condone killing a man. She'd taken the side of law and order for a reason. Her morals were far more shining than his. They always had been.

He didn't want her to know about the other side of his life.

"Stall Ms. Evers," John was saying. "Marlies is already out of the Netherlands, but Harry's not due to be transferred until the middle of May. Wait until after he's gone."

"Ten weeks is a long time to stall an investigation," Dan observed. "Alycia's going to think we have something to hide." Which they did, and it wasn't business anyone wanted traced back to CSIS. Or Canada.

"You'll think of a reason to give her," John said. He looked past Dan toward the door. "Well, well. Speak of the devil. You'd better think one up fast. Seems our after-hours meeting place has been compromised. Bruno won't be happy with you if an RCMP investigator turns into a regular."

Dan crooked his neck, taking a glance. Alycia stood inside the pub's entrance, scanning the tables. Judging by her business clothes and the briefcase, she'd come straight from work.

Her eyes met his. His stomach shot straight to his throat, where it lodged. God, she was so gorgeous.

"Sorry," he said to his boss.

John shrugged it off. "This is a public place. She's free to come here if she likes. Although I have to say, the Weasel doesn't really seem her style." He grabbed his coat. "Ms. Evers," he greeted her. "What a pleasant surprise. I wish I had time to talk, but my wife expects me home for dinner."

Alycia's cheeks dimpled as she smiled up at him. "Don't let me keep you."

John's straight, dignified back wove between the tables, as out of place in the sports pub as she was, at least to the casual observer. But people had layers, and John's were complex.

Alycia's were too. Dan played with his glass, still two-thirds full, curious—maybe hopeful—as to why she was here.

She slid into the seat across from him. "You aren't at all a hard man to track down," she said. "You must have skipped the class on evasion in spy school." She unwound her scarf, draping it over the back of the empty chair closest to her.

He'd used that same blue scarf to bind one of her hands to her headboard.

Once his thoughts went there, it was hard to redirect them. He had a mental flash of his hands on her naked buttocks while he thrust deep inside her and she begged him for more. Had she worn the scarf as a message? Had she tracked him down to collect on that debt?

The business attire suggested wishful thinking on his part. "I don't have any need for evasion," he replied. "I work in an office these days. My whereabouts aren't a state secret."

She combed her straight, blunt-cut hair with her fingers. The shining, cherry-brown swathe cascaded over the turtleneck collar of her sweater dress. The tips brushed her slight shoulders. "Good to know. So I can assume you never got back to me because you've been busy, not because you're avoiding me?"

This conversation could be headed in one of two directions. If she referred to the transcript, then yes, he'd been putting that off. As far as the other matter went... He'd picked up the phone at least a half dozen times. "Why would I avoid you?"

Electric blue eyes smoldered at him. "There are more productive games we could be playing than this, don't you think?"

She was right. The other night had been a good warm-up. Better than good. But the next round of play, one with her in control, would require some explaining on his part, and he couldn't predict how she'd react, which made him wary. He had scars from his field days and they weren't psychological.

"The transcript you asked for is tied up in another matter," he said. "It's going to be a few more weeks before I can get it to you."

As far as excuses went, this one was plausible. Evidence got tied up all the time. It was also the truth—up to a point. He waited to see if she bought it.

Those long, dark-tipped red lashes dropped to half-mast. Her brows formed a vee of annoyance. "You aren't getting cold feet on me, are you?"

Were they talking about the investigation or his willingness to let her give orders in bed?

"Why would I get cold feet?" he parried, opting for a response that could go either way.

She tilted her head. "Answering questions with questions... You're hiding something from me."

It was too easy to forget that she was an RCMP

inspector trained in interrogation when, in his head, she'd always be the girl with an enthusiasm for art, social causes, and full body massages. That Alycia had been straightforward. This one was not.

"Jesus, Allie," he said, exasperated by more than the wordplay. His testicles ached with confusion. "Could you please be more direct so I know what you're after?"

"What do you think I'm after?"

There she went, turning his tactics against him. If the conversation continued this way they'd be here a while. He pushed his unfinished beer away and signaled for the food waitress to come over.

"Can you bring us a plate of nachos?" he asked. When the waitress was gone, he refocused his attention on Alycia. "If you're looking for more of what I gave you the other night, then the answer is no, I'm not getting cold feet."

Glasses clinked as the bartender gathered the empties from tables nearby. He whistled while he worked, studiously intent on not listening in, which he was doing, so he and Bruno could have a good laugh at Dan's expense later. Bastards, both of them. Dan needed to find a new circle of friends.

Alycia leaned across their table, either unaware or uncaring that they had an audience. "You'd have to do what I tell you this time. You'd have to do the same things you asked me to do. Maybe you can't handle that."

Dan laughed. He couldn't help it. She sounded so certain. "If you really think I have issues with stroking myself while you watch, you're in for such a surprise."

The bartender fumbled his tray, barely managing to save the empty glasses carefully balanced for weight. Alycia's cheeks flamed a fire-engine red but her eyes remained on Dan's face. "Can you keep your voice down?"

Dan shot the bartender a hard look. He took the hint, his ear-to-ear grin speaking louder than words.

Once he was out of earshot, Dan addressed Alycia. "Tell me what you really want to know, then. Why did you track me down here? What didn't you dare ask me about at the office or over the phone?"

The color in her cheeks remained high. The determined way she stuck out her chin combined with the set of her jaw said he was about to get an honest answer, at least in part. "David believes you're going to get us into this investigation too deep to get out, but that you won't stick it out to the end—especially if we switch our focus from the target you'd intended."

She wasn't here about the debt, then. He was disappointed, but that ball remained in her court. If she wanted a repeat, she'd have to ask for it. "Where are you planning to focus?"

"The PMO is expressing reluctance to charge a minister. Since foreign countries are involved, the GAC concurs. Until we have irrefutable proof, we'd like to keep the matter domestic. We want to shift the investigation from the minister to his personal lawyer." Her dark blue eyes examined him. "Would you attend a meeting with Global Affairs and the Prime Minister's Office and give them a verbal report of what's on the transcript?"

Dan thought it over. He wanted to help her.

He wanted to protect his intelligence officer more. "I won't say where the information came from or reveal anything that might identify its source. I'll agree to name who the transcript incriminates but not what the incriminating evidence against them is. The PMO and GAC will have to wait, same as you."

A finely-arched eyebrow went up. "So you're willing to swear to a roomful of people, who have no love or trust for you, that you're telling the truth, yet offer them nothing but your word as a guarantee?"

"When you say it like that, you make it sound as if no one will believe me."

"And you make it sound as if anyone should." Alycia sighed. "But I'll take it."

The nachos arrived along with two side plates and napkins.

Dan was about to order her a drink but she stopped him. For the first time since she sat down she didn't meet his eyes. "I can't stay. I have plans later on."

Inside, a part of him died. The missing handful of condoms—the size of the box—crossed his mind. They hadn't discussed exclusivity, only how long since their last times had been.

Three years for her...

He pulled himself together. She wasn't rushing off to have sex with somebody else. She was, however, brushing him off. In the four days since he'd left her bedroom, something had happened. He didn't know what. There were too many possibilities, and maybe they were all for the best. He'd never been good for her. He'd drawn on all that fire she'd possessed to supplement what was lacking in him. She'd made him *feel*.

He'd been such a selfish bastard, taking everything she'd offered and giving nothing in return.

She stood, winding the blue scarf around her neck and sliding her arms into her coat, the slow, deliberate movements and bold, level gaze reminding him of her striptease—but in reverse. She didn't ask him to walk back to her place with her. She didn't suggest they go somewhere more private to collect on that debt. It was as if the other night had never happened, or made no lasting impression on her.

But he'd been there, so he wasn't buying the act.

"We're meeting with David and Global Affairs on Tuesday at the Prime Minister's Office. I'll email you the details," she said.

Then, with a lift of her hand, she walked away.

He dragged a nacho dripping with sour cream and salsa from underneath the melted cheese, not bothering with one of the plates, tracking her departure. He chewed without tasting, his thoughts morose. He'd once pursued excitement the way an addict chases his next fix.

Tonight, a weekend of drywall loomed ahead of him.

CHAPTER NINE

THE MEETING WITH THE PMO and GAC went as well as anyone could expect. They'd asked him questions. Dan had been evasive. It was all a formality.

In the end, they'd accepted his assurance on behalf of the CSIS director that the intelligence was solid. It was agreed that Patrick MacKenzie, Canada's Minister of National Defence, was to be advised to hire a civilian lawyer. Even though he was a government official, the Department of Justice wouldn't represent him in this matter.

Throughout the meeting Dan was hyper-aware of Alycia. No one else would know from her demeanor that she had anything other than a professional interest in him, but he wasn't anyone else, and he knew what signs to look for. Since she had a significant investment in the outcome of this meeting, she should have been hanging on his every word. Instead, she appeared to be only half-listening. She refused to meet his eyes, even when he was speaking directly to her. And the biggest of all—she didn't leap to his defense when the PMO made accusations of self-interest against his organization. Alycia was all about standing up for the underdog, and at this meeting, that was him.

He was intrigued by her behavior. The weekend had been long because he couldn't stop thinking of her. He'd considered calling, but until he figured out what had changed between them and why, he was keeping his distance.

She was one of two women in the room. The other was a senior member of the PMO's staff who appeared to be in her mid-to-late fifties, with a bright smile and stout, grandmotherly appearance. She cornered Alycia as the meeting wrapped up, asking her a question about her aunt and a fundraiser they were supposed to attend together. Dan missed Alycia's answer because David, the special prosecutor, approached him and asked to have a word in private.

"Let's go grab a coffee," David said.

Dan cast Alycia one last, sidelong look, not giving a damn what anyone thought about his interest in her, but she was still pretending not to pay any attention to him, so he followed David out of the building. She'd come to him when she was ready.

From Langevin Block they headed to a small coffee shop on a corner a few streets over. David held the glass door for a young woman in a short wool coat, black tights, and a miniskirt who gave him a casual onceover. Dan she ignored.

Good thing his self-esteem was healthy, because lately it was taking a beating.

Inside, the smell of warm brownies and fresh coffee hit him. The shop was L-shaped, with a counter and stools opposite the baristas and tables and chairs around the bend. David placed an order for two black house blends, and they grabbed a table in the farthest corner, out of sight of the door.

Dan snagged a seat that placed his back to the wall, his

curiosity raised. David was smart and didn't miss much. As a government lawyer, he knew what evidence he'd be permitted to use when prosecuting the case. During the meeting, he'd fielded a number of the questions directed at Dan, dismissing them as extraneous to the matter at hand. At the same time, he'd established to the PMO and GAC that CSIS, the RCMP, and the PPSC were working well together, thus easing any official concerns the PMO might have in that regard.

Dan didn't have to wait long to find out why David had asked for a word. The special prosecutor held the heavy porcelain cup to his lips with both hands and blew gently on the hot liquid's surface.

He inspected Dan over the rim. "Meredith Lively asked me to speak to you."

Dan couldn't begin to imagine what the Director of Special Prosecutions might want from him, but David looked uncomfortable about it, so this had to be good.

"She seems to think you might have a personal interest in her niece," David continued.

"You mean Alycia?" Dan had known of an aunt she was particularly close to, but he hadn't connected that Meredith to the Director of Special Prosecutions. He wondered if John knew the two women were related. And he was beginning to get a glimmer of where Alycia's abrupt coolness toward him originated. "Alycia and I knew each other in college. But that's not new information to you."

"Meredith says that Alycia was engaged to some larger-than-life, superhero doctor who was killed doing volunteer work in Sudan. You had a friend who was murdered in Sudan. Since that's an awfully big coincidence, I'm going to guess that your friend and her fiancé are one and the same. My next guess is that you and she knew each other a lot better than she led me to believe."

Dan studied David, who studied him back, his expression willfully bland. Meredith, was it? If they were on a first-name basis, then David was someone the Director held in high regard, meaning she'd assigned him to the case to minimize her niece's chances of failure. That was a positive sign—for Alycia's investigation. He, however, didn't like people knowing too much about his private business.

"You're free to assume whatever you like," he said. "So is your boss."

David held up his hands, palms out, in a mock-conciliatory gesture. "I'm just the messenger."

"The message being…?"

"She doesn't believe it would be good for Alycia's long-term career as an RCMP investigator to become involved with a CSIS intelligence officer."

Bingo. Alycia had told her aunt about him, and her aunt had planted doubts in her head. She thought he'd use Alycia for information, and Alycia had taken a step back to think—as well she should.

"I work in an office. My field days are behind me," he said. Until he knew what Alycia had told her aunt about him, he wasn't confirming or denying or getting bent out of shape. He was also fine with David thinking she was off-limits.

"Are those days ever really behind you?"

The question was fair. The answer? Somewhat murkier. Dan had sat in the Greasy Weasel only a few days ago, plotting a man's murder. If word of that ever reached Meredith's ears, it would prove awkward. "You can tell your boss the message was received."

"And?"

"And nothing," Dan said. "That's it." The legs on his chair stuttered against the tiled floor, catching in the grout as he stood. "Thanks for the coffee."

"Any time," David replied, cheerfully adjusting his glasses with his middle finger in a final salute.

As Dan made his way back to his office, he did some thinking. He usually kept a tight leash on his anger, but every once in a while it gave him the slip. This time it was on Alycia's behalf. She had every right to entertain second thoughts about him, but no one else got to change her mind for her. If she wanted nothing more to do with him outside of her investigation, then she could talk to him about it, and he'd understand.

Until then, he'd be the same selfish bastard he'd always been when it came to her.

Around eight o'clock that evening Dan called her from the intercom downstairs, unannounced, asking to be let in.

Alycia had wondered how long it might be before he arrived on her doorstep, seeking an explanation for her apparent loss of interest. She didn't have one. She'd pursued him, so what could she say?

Sorry. My aunt doesn't approve.

She wasn't a child. Her aunt was entitled to her opinions, but she couldn't make decisions for her.

And yet Alycia didn't need or want any commitments from Dan. All she wanted from him was some indication, no matter how slight, that she was worth pursuing too.

She raced around the living room, gathering up her laptop and a few loose papers before shutting them away in her office. While she didn't want to believe he'd go through her files, she did have a legal and moral obligation to protect the confidential information in her possession and saw no point in waving it under his nose. She knew what he was. He'd never lied to her about that.

She froze, her brain stumbling over that thought. Dan had never lied to her, period. She'd swear to it. Yes, he held back on her, but usually about things she didn't want to acknowledge—he had a sixth sense for picking up on weaknesses in others.

She, however, had learned her weaknesses a long time ago. She knew her strengths, too.

A soft rap on her front door had her running a nervous hand over her hair, smoothing it into place. She swung the door open and her heart lurched. He shouldered into the small entry, kicked the door shut behind him, and without uttering a word, cupped her face between his palms. Then he kissed her until she was weak-kneed and clinging to the front of his jacket, clutching handfuls of leather and breathing him in.

"Tell me right now that you don't want me here, and I'm gone," he said, his fingers still on her face.

She swayed on her feet, daring to hope. Maybe there was a connection, and possibly tenderness and affection, between them after all. The secret was in managing expectations, and she'd learned to set the bar low. He couldn't break her heart again if she didn't let him. The fact that he was here, on his own, was more than enough.

"I want you," she said.

His jacket and boots came off, left in a pile by the door. He lifted her into his arms, her fingers digging into his hair, elbows locked behind his shoulders, legs wrapped around his waist, and his hands supporting her weight. She kissed him, her mouth hungry on his.

They didn't make it to the bedroom. He hit the light

switch with his elbow, plunging her living room into semi-darkness. He tumbled her onto the sofa. She heard the rasp of his zipper, then felt his palms as they skated beneath the waist band of her yoga pants, tugging them down her legs. His thick erection nudged at her thigh.

So this was how he wanted it. Fast and furious, with no talking beforehand. Ready for him since the moment he stepped through the door, she was more than willing to oblige.

"Condom," she gasped.

"Right here."

He held one up, tearing the packet open with his teeth. In seconds, he had it on. Then he was inside her. He thrust. Groaned. Thrust again. She parted her knees and lifted her hips, taking him deeper, her fingers digging into the denim covering his rock-solid butt. A tingling began, deep in her belly, until it built to the point when she could no longer contain it. Tiny, pulsating muscles massaged his shaft, shooting out wave after wave of pleasure. She arched her back on a cry of mind-numbing release, wrapping one leg around his, digging her heel into the back of his thigh.

Dan had one hand braced on the sofa above her head, supporting his weight, and one foot on the floor. His whole body went stiff, then shook as he came. He collapsed half-on, half-off her, his weight heavy, although not uncomfortably so. Alycia could feel his heart pounding.

They were still almost fully clothed. Her pants were tangled around one ankle. Her shirt was shoved up to expose the sports bra she wore underneath. The fly of Dan's jeans flapped open and he had his underwear hauled aside. Both of them were breathing heavily.

He wiped her damp hair away from her face and kissed her forehead. His palm cupped her cheek, his thumb brushing her lips. "Sorry. I couldn't wait any longer. I was thinking about this all day."

Alycia skimmed her hands under his jeans. "Was this the only scenario you came up with? Not that I'm not complaining, mind you. Just wondering how much more energy I'll need."

The room was very quiet. Dan's face, shadowy above hers as she gazed up at him, shifted into a soft grin. "A few hours' worth at least."

Dan Hanson was a complicated man. She'd never grow tired of trying to figure him out.

Surrounded in the darkness of the bedroom, cocooned in the warmth of the bed, she trailed a lazy hand over his hip. He had more muscle on him than one might suspect, which stood to reason since there was a lot more to him overall than most people saw. And he still cared for her. He hadn't changed so much that she couldn't tell that.

But he didn't *want* to care, and that was what she couldn't figure out. What had she done wrong ten years ago? Had she been too clingy? Too needy? Too demanding or possessive?

She was none of those things anymore.

Her exploring hand bumped into a rough ridge of flesh along the lower part of his left ribcage, maybe six inches long, possibly more. She lingered there, rolling it beneath her fingertips. A knife wound. An old one, judging by the feel. She hadn't noticed it before only because he'd taken care not to let her discover it. But he wasn't hiding it from her right now.

She felt his eyes on her in the darkness, waiting to see

how she'd react. He'd gone very tense while she explored. Quiet. How many more scars did he have?

"How did you get this?" she asked, tapping the scar with the pad of her index finger.

"In a bar fight in Marrakesh six or seven years ago."

She processed that. If he'd wanted to lie, he'd have come up with something less disturbing. She appreciated that he didn't try to protect her from this, and she wasn't going to thank him by making a big deal out of something that was over and done with.

"Did you win?" she asked, trying her best to make light of it.

She felt his body relax slightly even as his arm tightened around her. "What do you think?"

"You did."

She was confident of it. He would have been underestimated because he wasn't big, intimidating, or openly aggressive. He wasn't reckless either. He'd have weighed the risks before entering a dangerous situation. A few scars would be nothing to him, simply the price to be paid for whatever he'd had to accomplish. No wonder CSIS recruited him.

Thank God those days were behind him. She had confidence in him, yes, but no one could control every aspect of danger, no matter how careful they were or harmless they seemed.

"You've traveled a lot," she said, changing the subject. "Tell me about your favorite place and what you loved about it."

"The Musandam Peninsula in Oman," he said without hesitation. "I loved the history of it, and the isolation. It's almost untouched by the outside world. The colors of the water surrounding it are amazing. Omanis are very low-key and traditional."

Alycia was riveted by this flash of insight into his personality. "What were you doing there?"

"Observing   smugglers.   Like   I   said—*almost* untouched."

"Don't you ever do anything strictly for fun?" she asked. When she thought back on it, she could see the pattern developing. Dan had worked hard in university. For six months, she'd been his one distraction. Even now, in his spare time, he occupied himself with physical labor.

"What makes you think that wasn't fun?"

He sounded so surprised, which made her laugh. Another insight for her to examine—he'd loved working as an intelligence officer.

Of course he had. He'd chosen it over her.

But Alycia no longer needed to be the center of anyone's universe, or for anyone to be the center of hers. She'd expected too much of him, and he'd made the right choice, and she wasn't blaming him for it anymore. Owning the responsibility for another person's happiness was too great a burden.

"Why did you give up being an intelligence officer?" she asked.

His response took longer this time. "I didn't give it up. I asked for a break. Part of my job was monitoring the psychological stress the people I worked with were under. I also had to think like our targets, and an extended period of putting yourself in their shoes—particularly when you don't share their line of thinking—takes a toll on a man. I saw mine coming."

Pragmatic as well as complicated.

"Now that you've been out for a while, would you go back to fieldwork?"

"If offered the right opportunity, I'd give it serious consideration." His chest rose and fell beneath her cheek as he spoke, the warmth of his breath stirring her hair. "Working in an office isn't anything I'd planned on doing forever. But I have a responsibility to the teams I currently handle. Their lives are more important than my job satisfaction."

His words held a warning—one she didn't need. She'd already learned she was on the low end of the spectrum of what was important to him. Besides, intelligence officers did count on their team leaders. They'd have few other people to trust.

She yawned, stretching, rubbing her legs against his, and changed the subject. "You need to show up here on a Friday so we can sleep in," she said, glancing at the clock with regret. "Having to go to work in a few hours is an inconvenience."

"I can see I've outworn my welcome." He kissed the side of her throat, making her reassess how much energy she had remaining against the coming demands of the day.

She caressed his calf with her toe, reluctant to say good-bye. "It's late. You don't have to leave."

"I do if either of us wants any sleep at all."

He flipped on the bedside lamp, then began gathering his scattered clothes off the floor. With the light on, she could see he had more scars—although none as serious as the long slash on his ribcage, which had been stitched up by someone unconcerned about appearances. He had another scar from a stab wound on his right shoulder, puckered, jagged, and angry, but the dimensions suggested the blade had been small.

The knife used on Terry would have been a lot bigger than that.

"Are you OK?" Dan asked, his voice far away and distorted.

The concern in it was what brought her back to the

bedroom. He had his arms in his shirtsleeves. The front was open, its tail hanging outside his unzipped jeans. Tousled brown hair stood on end. She was staring at him, and the expression in his dark-lashed, hazel eyes said he and his fancy psychology degree knew why. He'd had a solid reason for not wanting her to see those particular scars. He knew they'd be triggers.

The panicked sensation that had begun its slow crawl into her chest grew faint, then subsided. Reality returned. Dan wasn't Terry. He would never have walked into a war zone, mistakenly believing that the value of the good work he was doing outweighed any risks. He wasn't naïve and trusting.

He was a complicated, pragmatic realist who knew his own limitations.

"Never better," she replied, and discovered she was. This interlude with Dan—for that's all it was—was proving cathartic. She didn't need promises from him that he'd never keep.

He leaned over the bed and kissed her. "I'll be back on Friday," he said. "That way you can sleep in as long as you like."

You. Not *we.* Not a lie, but circumvention.

"Wear something pretty," she said lightly. "I plan to collect, and it had better be worth my while."

Tired as she was, even after he left she still couldn't sleep. One worrisome question continued to plague her. She wasn't asking anything of him that he wasn't willing to give. He'd come here tonight on his own and she'd played by his rules. So what made him reluctant to spend the whole night?

What was he hiding from her?

CHAPTER TEN

WHENEVER ALYCIA GOT THAT look on her face—as if her whole world were ending and she was falling apart—Dan began to smell roses.

No word of a lie. It freaked him out.

When he arrived at work—late—it was to find a representative from Global Affairs waiting for him. John was out of the office on business, so the GAC rep had been cooling his heels in Security for at least twenty minutes, and to say he was unhappy about it would be an understatement.

Dan led him to a conference room so they could speak in private, already fairly certain what this was about.

He wasn't disappointed.

"I want to know everything CSIS has on the defense minister," the man said.

Dan didn't hold back, although he did keep Lies's name to himself. Global Affairs wasn't interested in her anyway. All they wanted to know was how big the mess was and if it could be contained. Dan explained—again—that the minister, probably through a base commander in Canada, was arranging for perfectly good military weapons systems parts to be decommissioned and sold off as salvage. Those parts were then re-labeled and shipped through Europe, taking advantage of its open borders and common currency, to countries Canada officially didn't do business with because of its nuclear non-proliferation treaty.

The GAC rep's expression grew grimmer as the specifics unfolded.

"How long do we have before the Americans find out that Canadian parts are showing up on aircraft they probably manufactured?" he asked.

Sonofabitch.

Dan took a second to wrap his head around the question and think through his answer. That connection was one John had hoped the GAC wouldn't make. Not this soon. As the Original Equipment Manufacturer of a significant portion of this hemisphere's aircraft, most American contracts stated that replacement parts for any products they manufactured had to be purchased from the OEM or an authorized dealer. Even if a Canadian maintenance-and-repair contractor was authorized by an American OEM to produce parts, any that were decommissioned would no longer be covered by their agreement. And if foreign aircraft purchased from an American OEM were then being enhanced to nuclear capability using unauthorized parts produced in Canada...

"They'd already know," Dan was forced to admit. The spy world was small and information was constantly being exchanged within it.

"I'm going to drop this in your lap and let CSIS sort it out." The rep settled his hands on his thighs, propelling himself to his feet. "In the meantime, Global Affairs requests CSIS withhold any information that might drag more countries into this."

As he saw the rep out and made his way to his desk, Dan chose to look on the bright side. This solved one of his problems. He didn't have to try and stall Alycia. Not in this regard.

But she was already hinting around for him to spend the whole night with her, and while he was tempted, he hadn't yet been able to step over that line. She'd handled his physical scars better than he'd expected. Exposing her to his emotional ones when she had enough of her own would be stretching his luck.

She called him mid-afternoon, as soon as she got word from the GAC that CSIS could release any and all material pertaining to the case at its discretion.

"The next time you have one of these side meetings, I'd appreciate a heads-up," she said, sounding distinctly put out. "What am I supposed to do now, since you won't give me that transcript?"

Dan planted his feet on his desk and leaned back in his chair, happy to hear her voice even though it was filled with indignation. He could picture those crystal-blue eyes crackling in outrage, and it made him smile. She expressed so easily everything that he kept bottled inside.

The key to talking her down was to remain calm and give her nothing to react to. Unless he wanted a reaction from her, of course. He could push her as easily as she pushed him. The big difference was that when he did it, it was deliberate.

"*Can't*, not *won't*," he corrected her mildly. "Be creative. Why do you think no one wanted to take the defense minister on? What would be the next logical step?"

"I'm way ahead of you."

She sounded smug so he took a stab in the dark, just to

rattle her chain. "You're going after the lawyer, Mike Freeland."

A long pause said he'd guessed right.

"How do you *do* that?" she demanded.

"He's the logical choice," Dan said. "MacKenzie's position might protect him, but the people connected to him aren't quite as lucky. The GAC's objection to the case is over foreign relations and Freeland's a non-government, non-ex-pat player. With a little luck, you can connect him back to MacKenzie, which will make MacKenzie's involvement domestic. That takes away the GAC's objections, leaving only the PMO's to contend with, and David's a smart guy. He can work around them."

"If I tap Freeland's phones, how likely am I to get what I need to incriminate him?"

As if CSIS hadn't already tried that approach. "I can't say for certain, but my guess would be that if you do get it, you should be concerned. It will mean he believes he's untouchable too. Since these guys are arrogant, not careless, he'd have a good reason for that belief."

As he waited while she digested that, he heard a computer reminder ping on her end.

"I have a conference call starting in five minutes," she said. She didn't, however, hang up, so Dan waited for her to say what she had on her mind. "Are we still on for Friday night?" she asked.

"We are."

"Dinner first?"

Temptation hovered, a few inches out of his reach, but Alycia's anxiety wasn't his only trigger. Every time it looked like they might be getting too close, a tight, anxious knot formed in his stomach and he couldn't get the smell of roses out of his head.

"I'd better say no. I might be late."

After they said good-bye, he sat and stared at the wall. As much as he hated admitting to weakness, especially when it was his job to be strong, he needed to see a professional. He had to get his triggers under control.

Nothing much flustered John, so when Dan said he needed a few personal days to work through some issues, a long, slow blink of his eyes was the only obvious tell.

When Dan added he'd like to be transferred back into field work, however, John nodded wisely as if he'd seen that one coming. "It seems to me you might have left out some important details when you first asked to be taken off the MacKenzie case," he said, inviting Dan to take a chair on the other side of his desk. "Why don't you have a seat and give me the rest of the story. Only if you want to, of course. But maybe I can offer some insight."

Dan wasn't about to start sharing his feelings so he stuck to the facts. "I knew Alycia in university, before I joined CSIS. When I signed on, I broke off our relationship. A year after that, she started dating my best friend. Terry spoke to me about it first," he added, not wanting John to think they'd gone behind his back. "But I might have said I was OK with it when I wasn't."

"And then your friend was killed before you got to work things out with him."

It was so much worse than that.

"Not exactly. Terry went into Sudan because he knew I

was working there. He wouldn't have expected me to reveal classified intelligence, but he had every reason to believe I'd give him fair warning of trouble." Dan's hands were like ice. "The information I had might have saved his life, and I didn't give it to him. All I had to do was tell him to get out."

"CSIS was ordered to sit on that intelligence because the military wanted the rebels to know they were wasting their time going after hospitals. They also didn't want to reveal what resources Canada had in the area—there was a bigger battle shaping up nearby." John's hard gaze didn't quite mask his compassion. "If you'd told him to get out, he would have sounded the alarm. That's why the hospital wasn't alerted. No one had any way of knowing they'd execute one of the doctors."

"If he'd known of the attack, Terry still would never have left," Dan said. "Not without every single one of those kids, and too many of them couldn't be moved. That was the kind of man he was."

"And working with Ms. Evers has brought it all back for you too?"

Dan struggled for words. He'd never told anyone this part before. His feelings came into play, and he preferred keeping those to himself. "Again, not exactly. I have to ask myself why I chose to follow the rules even though I knew his life might be in danger."

"You think you sat on the intelligence because you were jealous of him?"

Hearing out loud words only ever whispered in the deepest, darkest regions of his head had cold sweat dripping the length of Dan's spine. He shrugged his shoulders, not knowing what else he could add.

"Here's the way I read the situation, based on what I know of you and what I knew about Sudan at the time,"

John said. He folded his hands on his desk, his gaze steady on Dan. "Things went to shit."

Dan cracked a dutiful smile. "No kidding."

"If you truly believe you sat on intelligence because you were jealous of a friend over a woman, then yes, you really do need to see a therapist, because I'm telling you, you're wrong. And I'll tell you something else." John leaned forward. "What you learned from that experience has been more valuable to you than you comprehend. You're one of the few men I know in our line of work who has a true moral center. You don't simply accept orders—you think everything through and weigh the consequences. You encourage that in your team members too. You tell them the rules, and your expectations of them, and then you leave them alone and allow them to do their jobs. Yours is the best team I have. So I have a question for you. If you could go back and do it over, would your decision be any different?"

"No," Dan said. He'd asked himself the same question more times than he could count, and the answer was always the same. "I don't really doubt the rightness of my decision as much as my motive for making it. That's what I can't get out of my head."

John's expression cleared as understanding dawned. "Let me ease your conscience in that regard. If you'd had all the facts—which nobody did—and there was a real chance to save your friend's life without sacrificing anyone else's, there's not a doubt in my mind that you would still have made the right moral choice. And it would have changed nothing, because your friend made his own choices when he went to a war zone."

"Terry believed there was good in everyone. He would never have imagined anyone targeting a children's hospital."

"Are you sitting there and diminishing the value of your friend's humanitarian work and his sacrifice by calling him naïve and stupid?" John asked. "Because those doctors were fully informed of what they were walking into. Saving other lives was more important to them than any personal danger to themselves."

When he put it that way, John made him feel low. "I know you're right, but it doesn't change how I feel. I don't know how to get past it on my own."

Raindrops pattered against the office window. "I'm no therapist, but I think you're trying to get past the wrong thing," John said slowly. "Ms. Evers was obviously someone important to you. She still is, if I'm reading things right. Have you considered that maybe it's not guilt you're feeling, but anger? With him, or her—possibly both?"

No way. John didn't know what he was talking about. Dan's head ached and his throat hurt. He wished for nothing more than this conversation to be over—but he'd started it, and now he had to finish. "I have no reason to be angry with either one of them."

"You're a trained psychologist. Is anger always a reasonable emotion? Of course it isn't," John said, not allowing him time to answer. "Yes, you should talk things over with a therapist. Take a week. Take two if you'd like. We can discuss your long-term plans to go back in the field after that."

Dan went back to his desk with a few new things to consider. Was he angry? If so, with whom?

He didn't know.

He did have to search for an excuse as to why he wouldn't be over to Alycia's Friday night, however, because until he sorted things out in his head, he didn't want her involved.

She didn't need his issues on top of her own.

Alycia could accept that something came up, even though Dan offered no explanation. He was with CSIS and that's how things worked.

A full week of radio silence, however, was not to be pardoned. When the second Friday rolled around, and she still hadn't heard from him and her calls went unreturned, she took a drive past his house.

Spring was around the corner. These were the gray days immediately before, when everything was melting and muddy and plants hadn't yet reawakened from winter's sleep. Dan's house was a saltbox built side-on to the street, two-storied on one side, single on the other. The last time she'd been here, it was dark and she hadn't noticed much except that it was small. She'd been wary of expressing too much interest in him or anything about him.

With good reason, it turned out.

She made a second pass, then parked across the street in front of his neighbor's house. Dusk had settled in, but Dan's lights weren't yet on. Maybe he wasn't home. She sat with the engine off, gripping the steering wheel in both hands, undecided about what to do next.

If only she could figure out what was going on in his head. He'd told her not to push him. That was one clue. But all things considered, she wasn't doing anything that could be construed as pushing, or at least pushing too hard—except perhaps sitting in front of his house and spying on him.

She was angry with him, frustrated with a situation

beyond her control, and impatient with herself for allowing him to keep doing this to her.

If this were only about her, however, she might be able to let it go and move on. It wasn't. Something was wrong with Dan, and that, she couldn't ignore. What did it take to emotionally derail the poster-boy for calm, cool self-control?

That was why she was here. To find out.

She could detect no movement inside the house. A dog slinked around a corner, darted between the house and the car in the driveway, and headed into the back yard. Since Dan didn't own a dog, she assumed it belonged to his neighbor.

She had to decide—did she go to the door, or did she go home?

Alycia conceded defeat. She was going home. Yes, she liked closure, but Dan's problems were his own. He'd dealt with them just fine until she'd come back into his life, so there was no question she was at least partly to blame. And an icy little voice in her heart whispered that if she was only one part of the problem, she might not want to know what the rest of it was.

She reached for the button to fire the ignition, so her head was turned away when the knock came on the car window. She jumped and let out a small scream, her hand flying to her chest.

Dan gestured for her to roll down the window, which she did, her heart still pounding. He had the collar of his flight jacket rolled up around his ears, his shoulders hunched against the raw wind. His hair was damp, and she caught a whiff of spicy soap, suggesting he'd just gotten out of the shower.

"You suck at surveillance," he said.

The threat of a heart attack passed, although expiring

from embarrassment remained a distinct possibility. "I'm out of practice."

He jerked his head toward the house. "Want to come inside? Or would you rather we talk out here?"

She searched his face. He sported a dark, five o'clock scruff. Calm, hazel eyes gazed into hers, and she lost some of her certainty. He didn't look like a man with a problem. He looked the same as always—sexy, with an undercurrent of danger that made her heart pound with anticipation. Maybe she'd overreacted. Maybe something really had come up and it was taking longer than expected. Espionage didn't follow a nine-to-five schedule.

Maybe she was the one who had problems.

She grabbed her purse off the seat beside her and yanked on the door handle, spilling five feet and two inches of irritation out of the car. Yes, she was going inside. Even if something had come up, and even if they hadn't made any commitments, he could have called.

She crossed the street beside him, taking two strides to his one. He opened the front door, then stepped back to allow her to enter first.

He'd extended the kitchen.

Alycia stopped short, staring in awe when sensor lights blinked on as she crossed the threshold from the entry. The ugly shag carpet in the former front room was gone, replaced by slate-gray ceramic flooring. The walls had been painted a pale gray with a slight hint of pink. He'd installed new windows and track lighting. The back wall at the far end of the kitchen and the mudroom were gone, replaced by two wide glass sliding doors that let in natural light and a view of the back yard. Soft gray wooden cupboards with inserts of opaque glass were offset by a two-toned glass backsplash. The counters sported granite-look laminate, with plenty of storage space underneath them. An engineered stone topper surrounded a separate prep sink for cooking in the island. New brushed stainless steel appliances completed the look.

It was gorgeous—more so because he would have done the majority of the work by himself. No wonder he'd brushed off her feeble offer of help. She could never have measured up to this standard.

Two high-backed wooden barstools tucked into the island were the only furniture in the otherwise open space. When she walked a bit farther, she saw that his living room set and television had been packed into the short part of the ell in what had once been the dining room, looking ragged and out of place in their shiny, upgraded surroundings. He'd probably buy new pieces once all the renovations were finished.

Dan stood next to her, saying nothing. He'd removed his jacket. The smell of fresh paint flooded the air. He had a splotch of white on the tail of his gray shirt, and it was embedded under his fingernails as if he hadn't been able to scrub it all off in the shower.

"This is amazing," she said, admiration spilling over despite her frustration with him. The man had to be part machine. Even his hobbies were practical. She spun on her heel, slamming a palm against his chest, catching him by surprise as she gave him a push. He staggered back a step before recovering his balance. "*This* is why you couldn't find the time to call me?"

"I've been seeing someone," Dan blurted out.

A red haze of fury cascaded over her eyes, obscuring her vision. It was the way he avoided her eyes as he confessed that lit the short fuse to her temper. It said he was ashamed to admit it.

As well he should be. She'd assumed that because she only ever slept with one person at a time he'd do the same, as a courtesy if for no other reason. "Do you lie awake at night, thinking up ways to end things between us that will hurt me the most? Are you an asshole to me on purpose?"

Dan's eyes went wide as if surprised she'd be so mad, then narrowed in understanding. "Jesus, Alycia. Give me some credit. Not *that* kind of seeing someone."

Now she was bewildered as well as enraged. "What other kind is there?"

A red flush began at the collar of his blue shaker-knit sweater and moved up his throat, spreading across his cheeks in dull blotches.

And suddenly, deflating, she figured it out. He wasn't sleeping with someone else. He was seeing a therapist. She had no idea why he, a trained psychologist, would be this uncomfortable about it. His job came with a high level of stress. Asking for help was hardly something to be ashamed of. She'd had therapy too. After her breakdown she'd had all kinds of support. Her family had been there for her. She'd come out stronger for it.

But Dan wasn't that close with his. His siblings were so much older that he was more like an only child. Not to mention, Dan's work was classified, and he was a loner by nature. He'd always had plenty of friends in university, but if pressed to name the ones who'd been closest to him, the list would be short. Even she hadn't made the cut. At the time she'd assumed it was because their relationship was different and she was more than a friend. Perhaps she'd been right. But in hindsight she saw that Dan had a different definition of friendship, and that was OK. Whatever problem he was dealing with, however, he shouldn't have to do it alone.

He was watching for her reaction to what to him was a bombshell. His shoulders were loose, his posture relaxed, maintaining a perfect gunfighter stance. Except for the red flush that was rapidly fading, to anyone else he'd appear calm.

She knew him so much better than that. He might have indifference down to an art, but she could *feel* the tension in him.

"Do you want to talk about it?" she asked, then berated herself for asking a question with such an obvious answer. "Of course you don't. If you did, you wouldn't be avoiding me."

"I'm not avoiding you. I've been working a few things out."

He reached for her coat, slipping it off her shoulders. She shook her arms free. While he went to stow her coat in the closet beside the front door, she dragged one of the kitchen stools to the opposite side of the island so they would have to actually look at each other.

Upon his return he made as if to stand at the counter, but Alycia patted the island topper in front of the unoccupied stool.

"If we're going to talk, then you're going to sit," she informed him. He wasn't the only one who knew a thing or two about interrogation and positions of power, and she wanted them to be on an equal footing. They weren't enemies. She couldn't say what they were—and that was the main reason why she was here.

He pushed the sleeves of his sweater halfway up to his elbows, slouched onto the edge of the stool, then rested folded arms on the island. Humor tugged at the corners of his mouth. Quiet, disarming hazel eyes locked with hers. "Is this better, Miss Bossy Pants?"

Not in the least. She couldn't shake the painful misgiving that, whatever his problem was, she played a key role. His use of the intimate nickname meant their past had been on his mind, and his seeing a therapist right after they'd begun sleeping together couldn't possibly bode well. Things were supposed to remain casual between them. Instead, they were becoming more and more complicated. And really—what else had she expected? They had a past.

He'd tried to warn her they were making a mistake while she, as always, had tried to make him react. She really did push him.

Her pulse drummed in her ears. The question that slipped off her tongue wasn't the one she'd intended to ask first, but it had bothered her since their first night of sex, and in her heart, she already knew the answer.

"Does the reason you're seeing someone have anything to do with why won't you spend the night in my bed?"

CHAPTER ELEVEN

DAN HAD ALWAYS ADMIRED her directness. He appreciated it even more now. It was a refreshing change from his regular routine of sifting through lies and deceit.

But a talent for directness didn't necessarily translate to a sincere desire for the truth, and he hated that he was about to unload his issues on her. His hang-ups weren't her fault, even if they were connected to her. He hoped she could make that distinction.

"I want you to listen to me and try not to take it too personally," he said, dodging her question. They'd get back to it in due time. "This is about how I feel, not whether I'm right or wrong. Can you do that for me?"

"You analyzed yourself, didn't you? I hope your therapist isn't a woman. She might take you for a mansplainer." She crossed her arms, settled her spine more comfortably against the back of the stool, and gave in. "Yes, I can do that."

She put on a good show, but the concern in her eyes spoke her true thoughts. She was genuinely worried for him, and he had to admit, it felt good to be on the receiving end for a change. He spent a large portion of his days looking out for other people. As his therapist—who wasn't a woman—had observed, while by nature he might be calm and cool under pressure, everyone had their weaknesses and maybe it was time he acknowledged his.

And his was Alycia. He wanted her, but not by default. She'd didn't love him anymore—he'd seen to that—and he didn't know how to earn back that love when he felt he no longer had any right to it.

He rubbed the back of his neck, working out the kinks he'd earned painting an upstairs bedroom and buying time while she waited for him to spit out whatever he planned to say.

"When my university advisor recommended me to CSIS recruiters, I saw an opportunity I might never get again, and I wanted so badly to take it, but it meant leaving you behind. I was fine with that because I thought you'd finish school, and by the time I came back, we'd be ready to move on to the next stage of our lives. Together. I really and truly believed you'd be waiting for me. Only the next thing I knew, Terry was sitting me down and asking if I'd be OK with the two of you seeing each other. I said yes, but I lied. I wasn't OK with it. I was pissed with you both."

Red crept from beneath the collar of her white turtleneck sweater and slowly spread to her cheeks. "You could have asked me to wait for you."

"Would you have said yes? The way I read it, you were too angry to try and understand how important the opportunity was to me." Her blue eyes flashed with hurt and indignation, and maybe—just maybe—a hint of guilt. She started to argue, no doubt to tell him he was wrong, but he stopped her. "Remember—this is about how I feel, not what I believe. I said I was pissed with you, but that doesn't mean I'm blaming you. I was definitely selfish.

And I wasn't as smart as I thought I was. We both had some growing up to do."

The old Alycia would have come right back at him, guns blazing. This newer, more mature version—the one who'd suffered her own losses, and had police training—appeared better able to see things from his perspective. Or at least more willing to try.

"Are you still angry with me?" she asked.

"Yeah," Dan admitted, and the confession felt amazing. "I guess I am. A part of me did believe that, if you'd really loved me, you would have waited—whether I asked you to or not. That's where these feelings come from."

Her gaze remained steady. "I'm not going to apologize for loving Terry. I needed a shoulder to cry on, and he was there for me. He earned his spot in my heart. You handed yours back. He never tried to replace you. You made us both believe that you didn't care."

That might be true, but Terry had known the unspoken guy rule that friends didn't date their friends' exes. The moment he first approached Dan about seeing Alycia, Dan lost two people he'd loved and trusted. And yes, he'd felt betrayed by them both. He'd broken up with Alycia and she'd been the injured party. No matter how he might feel, he had no right to blame her. But Terry should have known how he'd feel. And Terry had known—it was why he'd asked for permission. When Dan gave it to him, it absolved him of guilt.

No one was perfect. Not even saints.

Dan wasn't about to say any of that to Alycia, however. As much as it ate at him, she'd loved Terry, and he had to accept it.

"Fair enough," he acknowledged. "And it all lays the groundwork. Not long after he told me you two were getting married, I got my hands on intelligence revealing that his hospital was about to be targeted. When I took it to my team leader I was ordered to sit on it. There were rumors of an uprising, and the military didn't want the rebels to know what kind of force Canada had in the area. No matter how many ways I look at it, I would have made the same decision not to tell him. It was the right one. I know it. I believe it. If word had gotten out, the body count might have been in the thousands. But that doesn't change how I felt. How I *feel*. And I feel as if a part of me was glad that I didn't have to warn him. When I'm with you I feel guilty as hell. You remind me I'm not a very good human being."

"Is that why you can't fall asleep when you're with me?" Alycia's eyes softened with sympathy, as if all the pieces of a difficult puzzle had finally locked into place. "For a long time I never spent the whole night with anyone either. I used to have terrible nightmares. I'd wake up soaked in cold sweat. It took me years to get over the feeling that if I'd only tried harder to convince him not to go, I might have saved him."

If Dan planned to be honest with her, then this was his opportunity to lay it all out in the open. He might not get another. "I hated him for being smart enough to ask you to wait for him."

"You were right not to ask. I wouldn't have waited for you," Alycia said, her admission a painful jab to his gut. "You were two different men, and the situations were different."

"He was always better than me." He heard how petulant that sounded, even if it was the truth, and he winced.

Some of the softness in her eyes disappeared. She tilted her head to one side, the deep red of her hair sweeping her shoulder. "Is that what you believe or how you feel?"

"Believe," he decided, after a second of honest consideration. Terry hadn't been perfect, but he was a remarkable person, larger than life in so many ways.

But when it came to their friendship, Dan couldn't help feeling he'd gotten the shitty end of the stick—and having those negative feelings about someone like Terry was wrong, especially since Dan had done plenty of things that he wasn't proud of and would never want his mother to find out about.

"If you believe that, then you're mistaken. You didn't need me," she said gently. "That's why I wouldn't have waited for you, and what made me so angry. You never needed to discuss your decisions with anyone—you joining CSIS without talking to me first is an excellent example—because you've never had any doubts about the choices you make. You might feel guilty about being angry with Terry, but all you're really guilty of is having human emotions. Which I'm sure comes as a complete shock to you." Her cheeks dimpled briefly before she turned serious again. "Here's what I believe. If you'd known for certain Terry would die, not even a direct order would have kept you from warning him—and the warning would have been wasted. You know that as well as I do. He wasn't going to run. He cared more for helping those children than he did about saving himself. More than he cared about me. And I was angry with him too. I got over it. So will you."

Dan's throat had gone tight and scratchy, making his voice come out harsh. "You give me more credit than I deserve."

"You don't give yourself enough." She gave him a long, considering look. "Where does all of this leave you and me?"

Dan wasn't sure. He wanted her as much as he ever had. More. She was so freaking pretty. She had so much inner strength, and spoke to him bluntly in a way few people dared. Having her sitting here in his kitchen, and looking at him the way she was now, filled him with longing.

But they were no longer students with their futures unfolding before them. They had careers that didn't quite mesh. Her aunt had made a smart call on that. He'd done so many things he couldn't tell Alycia about—things he'd still have to do—and he didn't believe he'd be right for her anymore. Not professionally and certainly not personally. At a few weeks shy of thirty-three, kids had to be on her mind, and he couldn't begin to imagine what kind of role model he'd be. Besides, as a teenager with much older siblings, he'd done his fair share of babysitting nieces and nephews. Kids were a major responsibility. He'd do some poor tyke a favor and keep his lifestyle—and his DNA—to himself.

"I've asked John to send me back into the field," he said. "So you tell me. Where do you think that leaves us?"

She slid off her stool, the sole of first one knee-high leather boot striking the tile, then the other. She walked around the end of the island, a tiny bundle of colorful flame. She nudged his knees apart and pushed her hips between them, easing her arms around his neck. She drew his forehead against hers and peered into his eyes.

"You aren't getting off that easy," she said. "I'm not dwelling on things that can't be changed. Neither are you. We both know life is too short to spend it all on regret. And I'm not afraid of the work you do. But let me make something clear. I don't have a problem with you being too busy to spend time with me. I get it. It happens. If you want to go back to gathering intelligence, that's up to you.

However, just because we aren't making any commitments doesn't mean you get to make me a promise and not follow through, especially without any explanation. You told me we'd spend last Friday night together, and you missed it. I'm taking a raincheck tonight."

A laugh built inside him, his first real one in days. She really did know her own mind. If no one else got to change it for her, then neither did he.

His hands spanned her waist. "What do we call this?" he asked, just to be sure. And maybe to get a rise out of her. He liked her when she was spitting fire, all indignant. "A booty call? Friends with benefits? Casual sex?"

Her dimples flashed as her lips briefly brushed his in a slow slide that had him burning. "We aren't calling it anything. Tonight it'll be an evening of take-out and movies on Netflix. We'll put the pajama party on hold, because if anyone has to crawl out of a warm bed and head out into the cold after sex, it's going to be you."

His brain snagged on the words *warm bed* and *sex*. An image of Alycia pressed to his pillow, her hair swept away from her face, looking back at him with those amazing blue eyes while he knelt behind her with his hands on her naked hips, thrusting deep inside her, hijacked his brain.

He cupped her face in his palms, brushing his thumbs over the corners of her mouth. Desire rasped against a heart that was lighter now for having made his confession. It wouldn't take much to persuade her. They might not know what this was or how it would end, but they both liked the sex. His bed might be the best place for them to spend their first entire night together. He could consider it therapy.

It would be so easy…

"Maybe we should negotiate tonight's entertainment,"

he began. "I'm OK with ordering take-out, but I don't have a subscription to Netflix. And since I don't own pajamas, I—"

The front doorbell rang, cutting him off mid-sentence.

"Don't move," Dan ordered her.

She leaned on the island, watching him cross the long, empty room and pass through the archway that led to the front door. He'd dumped a lot on her, not all of it fair. At least not in her opinion.

But she wanted to be fair to him.

Her job was to investigate people who weren't what they seemed on the surface, so it gave her a rough idea of what his work entailed and the toll it could take. While he wasn't above the law, he didn't answer to it either. He operated in a gray area that could destroy him if he wasn't careful.

However, Dan was the most cautious man she'd ever met. He did nothing without thinking it through. It might not feel like it to him—truthfully, to her either—but when she took a step back and removed her emotions, she too believed he'd done the right thing in Sudan. If people had died because he'd tried to save someone who'd known the risks, something inside him would have died too. That he had all of these unresolved feelings, even if they were difficult for him to deal with, meant he at least still had a conscience. He could *feel*.

But her expectations of him had been too high once before. They didn't need to complicate things by giving whatever this was a name. They weren't falling in love again. Their past was messy enough. And if Dan was intent on going back into the field, well, her life no longer revolved around men.

"I have company," she heard him say. "An RCMP investigator is here."

It had to be someone from CSIS for him to give up that information. She wondered who would be coming to his house on a Friday night. And what could be so important.

"I'll come back another time."

The second voice was deeper than Dan's, although equally self-assured. He sounded like someone used to taking charge.

"No need. Just giving you a heads-up. Come in."

The newcomer was taller than Dan, but stockier. None of it was fat. He was in his early thirties, and while attractive, the slight crook in his nose gave his face added character. He had sandy-colored hair and a direct gaze that saw everything. His suit and overcoat, and general bearing, suggested he came from money. His clothes were expensive but didn't shout the fact.

He couldn't quite hide his surprise when he saw her. She caught the break in his stride and the tiny jerk of his shoulders, as if something had pulled him up short. She assumed it was because she was a woman. Being a female investigator often earned her that reaction, and she was well beyond being offended by it. Under-estimation usually worked to her advantage.

"Alycia, meet Garrett Downing," Dan said. "Garrett is a government program officer. He's currently working out of Sierra Leone." He rested a hand on the other man's shoulder. "Garrett, Alycia Evers is the investigator working on the case against Patrick MacKenzie."

Alycia and Garrett shook hands. "It's nice to meet you," she said, smiling up at him. He had nice eyes—serious but kind. But even as she decided she liked him, her mind was busy connecting the dots. Where did he fit into the investigation?

"Likewise." If Garrett thought it odd that the RCMP investigator was at Dan's place on a Friday night, he didn't let on. He returned her smile, then spoke to Dan. "John suggested I stop by. Sorry if I'm interrupting. He didn't tell me Ms. Evers would be here."

"It's OK. Alycia can be brought up to date."

"You're in Sierra Leone right now?" Alycia asked. "That must be so interesting. What other places have you been?"

"Don't answer that one," Dan interrupted. "She's fishing for information she was already told she couldn't have."

"Ah." Garrett nodded sagely. "She's after your sources."

"Just doing my job." Alycia smiled as she conceded defeat. If Garrett was the officer who'd been working in the Netherlands, he wasn't about to give it away now.

"Garrett helps set up and oversee relief programs in third world countries," Dan said. "Those programs might be compromised if his name should ever be connected to intelligence reports gathered from the countries he supports. Something for you to keep in mind while you're 'doing your job.'"

"Duly noted." And Alycia was suitably impressed. She'd known intelligence officers often took on multiple roles as part of their cover stories. She hadn't considered one of those might be humanitarian aid.

Dan relinquished his stool to Garrett, got three beers from the fridge, and distributed them, setting his on the island. Then he dragged a gray butterfly chair from the former dining room, now serving as a home for his flat screen TV. He parked the chair next to Alycia's and picked up his beer, twisting the cap off. "OK. Give me what you've got."

Garrett took a sip from his bottle and looked at the label with an expression of deep satisfaction. "Canadian brew. How I've missed you." Then he looked at Dan. "I've got confirmation from a friend in RAW that Canadian aircraft parts are being used on Pakistani aircraft."

"What's RAW?" Alycia asked.

"India's Research and Analysis Wing. They specialize in counter-terrorism and foreign intelligence," Garrett explained.

She digested that and couldn't see the importance. "You already knew those parts were going to Pakistan. It only makes sense they'd install them on their aircraft."

"But now the rest of the world knows it, too."

Alycia still didn't get it. "So what? Canada didn't sell them those parts. They would have come from a third party."

Dan answered her this time. "If it can be proven the parts came from the Canadian Minister of National Defence, even indirectly, or through a Canadian ex-pat such as Bernard Vanderloord, who has connections to him, Canada has an international incident on its hands. Those Pakistani aircraft are manufactured by the Americans. And the American manufacturers are not going to be happy. They're going to start looking around for what other countries might have purchased Canadian-manufactured parts for aircraft they own the maintenance rights to."

"I don't understand what any of this means," Alycia admitted. But obviously, it meant something important.

"It's a big reason why the PMO and Global Affairs don't want to press charges against MacKenzie," Dan said. "Global Affairs is going to have to respond to any international questions. If the Canadian government acknowledges that our defense minister is involved, then Canada has a degree of culpability for the end use of those parts. The last thing the PMO wants is for Canada to be held accountable for the actions of a hostile nation."

Now she got why Dan had told her she needed to bring the connection back to Canadian soil and stay away from Vanderloord and the Netherlands. MacKenzie really was untouchable—unless she found the connection between MacKenzie and Mike Freeland, the lawyer. It would be helpful if Dan was more cooperative, but she'd have to accept that when work was involved, their loyalties lay in different directions. He could separate business and pleasure. She didn't have that same faith in herself. She was too new to her position, and wanting to make a name for herself.

CSIS did not make the best bedfellow. Her aunt had tried to warn her of that. Dan wouldn't give her anything that didn't suit John Carmichael's purpose, and she didn't know what that was.

She listened, quietly playing with her unopened drink, while the two men exchanged other information. Dan seemed genuinely interested in the relief work Garrett was involved in, but she couldn't figure out the real connection between CSIS and orphanages. She didn't want to believe Canada could stoop so low as to use innocent children as some sort of bargaining chip. But the careful way Dan worded his questions left her convinced there was something he didn't want her to know, and her suspicions took a dark turn.

Garrett caught the look on her face.

"I bet Dan's never mentioned he donates to children's missions every year," he said, solving the mystery. "I'm here to hit him up. That's why he's asking so many questions. He wants to make sure his money's well spent."

The tips of Dan's ears turned a bright red. "I wasn't planning on mentioning it either," he muttered to Garrett.

"You'd rather have an RCMP investigator think you use children as spies? Because that's where her thoughts were going," the other man pointed out.

Dan tilted the lip of his beer bottle in Garrett's direction before taking a drink, not saying a word, and Alycia's heart melted. Dan supported a cause Terry had been passionate about, showing how deep his complex layers truly ran. How private he was. To think he believed he could consciously do harm to someone he loved…

How was it possible to be so frustrated and impressed by him all at once?

Garrett didn't stay long after that. From what Alycia pieced together, he had a new wife waiting for him in Nova Scotia, and he was anxious to get back to her. His plane left at ten.

"I've got about a half hour to make the gate for my flight," he said, finishing his beer. He glanced at his watch. "My taxi should be here any moment." A horn blared in the driveway. "And that would be it."

After Garrett left, Dan took his phone out of his back pocket. "I promised to feed you. Chinese OK?"

"Fine."

Her stomach, however, rebelled. She didn't care about food. She put her untouched beer back in the fridge while he placed the order, then stood at the glass doors staring into the night.

The past few hours had been so very enlightening. She knew more about Dan now than she had the entire time they'd gone out together—which, looking back, hadn't been very long. She'd been so in love it had seemed like forever. Had she ever known him as well as she'd once believed?

The answer was a resounding yes. She might not have known his life goals, but she'd known who he was inside. No matter how complicated he was, Dan knew right from wrong. He was loyal—that much was obvious from the way he protected his team, as well as his friend's memory.

He'd thought she'd be loyal too. That she would wait for him. No, he'd *believed* it. Her throat ached around a hard lump—not quite of regret, but something close to it. He might have hurt her, but she'd also hurt him.

So how did they avoid hurting each other again?

CHAPTER TWELVE

DOWNING'S ARRIVAL HAD KILLED the mood.

Dan was OK with that, simply relieved to be able to enjoy Alycia's presence with a clear conscience for a change. He'd unloaded his secrets and she'd been understanding. But her frown indicated that she was thinking too hard, and he couldn't have that. Putting his past to bed wasn't about bringing her down. He wanted her to be happy.

It was all he'd ever wanted for her.

He waved a hand in front of her face. "Hello? Earth to Alycia."

Wide, electric-blue eyes swiveled toward him. "When did you get a dog?"

Well. That put him in his place.

He bit back a grin as he looked past her shoulder, already knowing what he would see. The new glass doors framed the neighbor's Doberman, lit up in a splash of light from his kitchen, its ass in the air and front legs busily burying something or other in the soft dirt beneath his shrubs.

"It came with the house," he said.

"It's making a mess of your lawn. If this is an ongoing

problem in the neighborhood, you should call Animal Control and complain."

He'd come to accept that the owner wasn't going to take responsibility and decided it was past time to teach him a lesson. "I'm not reporting a dog for being a dog. Hang on a sec."

He opened a drawer and rooted around for a stick of beef jerky, then slid back one of the doors and stepped into the yard. It took only a little coaxing to lure the dog closer. It was more of a pup, friendly and eager for attention. Dan scratched it under its ears, playing with it for a few minutes, then hooked a long leash to the animal's collar. The leash was tethered to a metal tee he'd driven into the ground. He'd also bought a small bag of dog food and a couple of bowls. He set out water and kibble, then went back in the house, ignoring its whining and reproachful eyes.

"You brought this on yourself, big guy," he said as he closed the door. The dog barked in protest, but when that earned no reaction, it stuck its nose in the bowl of food and snuffled around.

"You can't just keep someone's dog," Alycia said.

Dan shrugged. "Sure I can. Isn't possession nine-tenths of the law?"

"Not really, no."

"Relax. I'm not planning to keep it forever. Only long enough to prove a point."

She gave him the type of look that usually preceded a stern talking-to, but the sharp peal of the doorbell signaled their food had arrived, and he was saved.

He paid for the delivery, then set the warm bags on the kitchen counter. Since sex was definitely off the table, at least until after the dog's owner showed up—which he would—they might as well eat their meal.

"Plates are in that cupboard," he said, pointing to the one closest to the dishwasher as he got out the flatware and napkins.

Somewhere, in one of the drawers, he knew he had candles. Alycia had always liked dinners at home to be nice, and he had no problem making an extra effort to please her. It beat eating beans out of a can heated over a campfire. There were a few things about field work—and Boy Scouts—that he didn't miss.

They'd have to sit at the island, however. Until now a dining room table had seemed a pointless investment for a house he planned to flip. When they'd dished up the food, he took the seat from where he could best watch the back yard.

They were finishing the last of the Peking Duck when Dan caught movement outside, in the shadows. He set down his fork and pretended to go to the sink. From there, he edged toward the glass doors. He slid the door open on its track and dashed into the yard too quick for his neighbor to dart away. He grabbed him by the back of his jacket, lifted him off his feet, and brought him onto the top of the deck. The pup bounced around their legs, barking with excitement, its tail beating against one of Dan's shins.

The boy was maybe twelve years of age, with scared but determined eyes and brown hair too long to keep tidy. Rather than struggling he tried to unzip his jacket and wiggle free, but Dan was wise to that trick. He shifted his hold to the boy's thin upper arm.

"You and I are long overdue for a talk," Dan said.

"I want my dog back. If you don't untie him, I'm calling the police."

"I'll save you the trouble. See the lady sitting in my kitchen? She's a police officer. Go ahead and make a complaint," Dan said. Alycia, perched on her stool with her cheek propped on her hand, appeared to be enjoying the show. She waggled her fingers and the boy stuck out his tongue.

"That's not a cop. That's a girl."

"Don't make me come out there and show you my badge," Alycia said. "I don't want to have to place you under arrest for trespassing and juvenile male chauvinism. You gentlemen resolve this matter yourselves."

Dan shook his head at his young neighbor. "You have a lot to learn about girls, Liam. They'll hit a guy first, especially if they don't like his attitude, and they make really mean cops if you disrespect them. Now. How badly do you want your dog back?"

"Keep him. I'll play with him when you aren't home."

The kid was clever. Dan pretended to think over his proposition. "I'd be fine with that arrangement, except I can't leave him outdoors to run loose when I'm at work. He might start digging holes and taking craps in other people's yards, and that sends a bad message to the neighbors. But, since you're willing to give him away, I've got a better idea. Want a dog?" he called to Alycia.

"I'd love one," she said. "He's perfect. I'm going to name him Princess. He'd really rock one of those fuzzy pink dog sweaters."

"You guys are hysterical." Liam took a half-hearted swipe at Dan's leg with the toe of one sneaker. "Give me back my dog."

"As soon as you pick up the mess he made in my yard."

The kid and his lower lip took the meaning of sullen to new heights. "I don't have anything to pick it up with."

"This is your lucky day. Alycia, want to grab us a couple of those poop bags from the drawer next to the sink?" She hopped off her stool and a few minutes later, passed him a handful of biodegradable plastic. "I happen to be in a good mood, and I like your dog, so I'm going to help you."

"Bite me," Liam said, but his heart wasn't in it. Dan could tell he recognized a face-saving compromise when he saw it.

By the time they'd finished and the bags were disposed of in the garbage bin at the side of the house, Alycia had tidied the kitchen and was watching TV in the other room. She'd taken off her boots and curled up on his sofa. Dan washed his hands at the sink, took a quick look through his window to make sure the kid didn't try to set his trashcan on fire, and then went to join her.

"You really have a way with children," she said. Her eyes danced.

"You're a fine one to talk. Princess? Fuzzy pink dog sweater?"

"We'd make terrible parents."

"Speak for yourself," Dan said, curious to see what she thought of his true potential. "I'd be amazing."

"Of course you would." But she sounded as if she were humoring him, confirming his own suspicions regarding his abilities in that area—he wasn't father material. Got it. "You know that dog poo is going to wind up inside a flaming paper bag on your doorstep, right?"

"I'll take that chance." Dan eased an arm along the back of the sofa and inched closer until she was nestled against him, her head on his shoulder. "Except for the attitude, he's not a bad kid. His dad is a single parent and a nurse who works a lot of night shifts. He got the dog to keep Liam company when he's home by himself. Unfortunately, he glossed over the lessons on dog owner responsibility and how not to annoy the neighbors."

"Liam seems bright. He'll figure it out."

"What are we watching?"

"A documentary on art theft."

Dan groaned a half-hearted protest. "But the hockey game's coming on."

"You had all week to watch television. This is my first chance."

He didn't give a damn about the game, or art theft either. He watched her, perfectly content. Twenty minutes into the show, however, her head slid from his shoulder to his chest. One arm hung slack at her side. She was asleep. He grabbed the remote and switched the channel.

After another hour passed and the game was in its third period, he was torn. She hadn't planned to stay, and yet she was too tired to leave. He could carry her upstairs and deal with it in the morning, or he could wake her up and see if she preferred him to drive her home.

Before he could decide, she stirred on her own.

"You don't have to do that. I'll be fine," she said when he offered to drive her. She hid a yawn with the back of her hand. "It's not even midnight."

It was a Friday night after a long work week. She'd been angry enough to come over here to see what he was up to, so chances were good she hadn't been getting much sleep. Rage had that effect on people. He wasn't letting her get behind the wheel of a car when she couldn't stay awake through an entire TV episode, no matter how dull it was.

"You've got one of two choices, Bossy Pants. Either I drive you home or you spend the night."

"The whole night?" She batted blue eyes still heavy-lidded with sleep. "What an honor."

Sarcasm. Cute. "You really think I'd toss a hot woman out of a warm bed?"

"No. But you might wish you could. That's even worse."

In the past they'd spent plenty of long nights together, then lingered in bed in the morning for hours. Avoiding old patterns was going to be hard, and they couldn't do it forever. Or even right now.

The trick wasn't so much to avoid the old patterns, but to overlay them with new ones. "Not if we set up the ground rules." He twisted a lock of her hair around his finger and gave a light tug. "First, no leaving girly stuff in my bathroom."

"Fine. You can't leave girly stuff in mine, either."

"Deal. Second. No talking business on weekends."

"Forget that. We'd run out of things to say in less than an hour. Let's settle on no talking business in bed."

Dan pretended to think, enjoying this game. "I'm good with that. On to rule three. Whoever wakes up first has to make breakfast."

"You underestimate how long I can sleep in on a weekend."

"Not really," Dan said. "You're a terrible cook, and I refuse to live on cold cereal and egg-white omelets. So the fourth rule applies to whoever's hosting the pajama party—the fridge has to be stocked for the morning."

She snuggled in closer, her cheek and one hand pressed to his chest. He rubbed the heel of his palm up and down her narrow back. "I'd argue that my culinary skills have improved, but I'm willing to take the hit to my pride as long as the stocked fridge includes fresh fruit and vegetables."

"Any other rules you want to add?"

"No. Yes." Her fingers curled in his shirt. "Aside from common courtesy, no unreasonable expectations. We each put our own career and needs first. If one of us has a problem, we say so. And when things run their course, they're over."

"You're such a romantic." Dan kissed the crown of her head, inhaling the soft scent of her girly shampoo with appreciation. Given the right incentives, he might be willing to bend on the bathroom rule. "I'm feeling generous. Since you're the one sleeping over, you get to decide on tonight's next activity."

"I can't help but feel that your generosity's self-serving, and while I'm wide awake now, I'm also tired and a little lazy. You, on the other hand, seem pretty energetic. I believe you owe me a striptease."

Dan heard the hint of a dare, although the joke was on her. This was definitely a break with tradition, and he was all in. "Never be let it said that I don't pay my debts. The neighborhood's rated PG, though, so we're going to have to take this show upstairs."

He stood, rolling her off the sofa and onto her feet, then scooped her up with one arm and hefted her over his shoulder. He planted his free hand on her ass to hold her steady. She didn't weigh much.

She shrieked with laughter, grabbing his belt. "Don't you dare drop me!"

"No danger of that."

He took the stairs two at a time. At the second-floor landing, a narrow hall led to three bedrooms and a main bath. He flipped on the hall light on his way to the main bedroom, the last door on the right. The room was in shadows. He'd invested in a queen-size bed. He heaved her into the middle. She bounced a few times, her hair in her eyes, still laughing as she swept it aside.

"Light on or off?" he inquired.

"Off," she said, propping herself on her elbows as she gazed up at him. "But leave the door open so I can see. I don't want to miss anything." She paused. "Are you really going to go through with this?"

"Of course I am. You said anything I did to you, you got to do to me."

"Keeping our respective plumbing in mind," she reminded him.

"Hell yes. That should really go without saying." He hooked his thumbs in his pockets and widened his stance, giving his best impression of a male underwear model. "So go ahead. Start giving instructions. I'm waiting."

She bit her lower lip. "You made giving orders look easy."

He chose to take that as a compliment. "Really, Bossy Pants? You're complaining because I'm not the one in charge? We can take care of that."

"No, no. I'm pointing something out to you, that's all." She sat upright on the bed, folding her stockinged feet under her thighs and cupping her bent knees in her palms. "Take off your shoes and socks. But make it look sexy."

Dan kicked off one shoe, then toed off the other. He turned his back to her, bent down, and removed his socks. He wiggled his ass and she started giggling again.

"It's hard to make taking socks off look sexy," he complained. "Give me a minute. I'm just getting started."

He shot his best attempt at a smoldering glance over his shoulder and peeled off his sweater. He twirled it above his head, pivoted on one heel, and tossed it onto the bed. Alycia rolled to her side, buried her face in the thick comforter, and howled with laughter. The sound filled the bedroom, and for a second, the world ground to a halt.

This.

This was what his life had been missing, and what he'd been so afraid he'd stolen from her. The warmth. The sunshine. The *fun.* All work and no play had made Dan a really, really dull boy—he had an entire team of people who told him so on a regular basis—and he'd never wanted that for her. He loved her so much his chest ached with the effort to contain it.

She lifted her head. Tears streamed down her cheeks. "If only John Carmichael could see you right now," she gasped out.

Dan managed to keep his tone light. "He'd have to pay me a lot more than he does."

She flipped onto her back, her eyes growing thoughtful as she examined his face. "Something's wrong. What's the matter?"

Not a thing. If anything, having her here was too perfect. "You tell me. I got rave reviews from the local Ladies' Auxiliary, a half-dozen propositions, and yet you're making fun of me."

"That's the reason, right there," she said. "This is one of those things that men and women view differently. If a roomful of men are watching a stripper, chances are good they're getting turned on by it. To them it's an individual experience. A roomful of women, on the other hand, are talking and laughing, making jokes about it. It's a night out with the girls. They're after the entertainment, the titillation, not the thrill. I can't take this seriously."

"I guess we have a problem. You're supposed to do to me what I did to you."

"If the objective is to turn each other on, then the biggest problem is our approach. *How* we go about it. You think like a man, so you're more likely to find a striptease sexy. But I'm a woman, and I'm more inclined to find it entertaining. You thought it was hot watching me touch myself. Fine, I liked doing that too," she admitted. Her gaze dropped to his bulging fly. Hunger entered her eyes. "But I find it a lot hotter to be touching you."

His brain shot to a visual image of her on her knees on his bed, taking him in her mouth. "That's not such a great idea. If you touch me right now, there won't be any more problems with our approach for at least another twenty minutes." He adjusted his package, which was hard, uncomfortable, and incredibly eager behind the restraint of his zipper. "Why don't we compromise and you tell me how you'd like me to touch you instead?"

She tugged at the inside of her lower lip with her teeth. He could hear the mental gears grinding as she thought it over. "I want you to touch me as if you can't keep your hands off me," she announced. Her gaze sharpened, homing in on his face. "And then I plan to touch you. This is supposed to be my night."

"The sacrifices I'm willing to make…" He slid down his zipper and freed himself from his jeans with a sigh of relief. He shucked out of the last of his clothes. "A man's gotta do what a man's gotta do."

"You're very selfless," she congratulated him.

"And you're fully dressed." He stretched out beside her on the bed, propping his head on one hand. The other one went to the buttons on the front of her blouse. "I can fix that for you."

"Dan Hanson—fixer of fully-clothed women," she teased. "You could put that on a business card."

"What—and have the Ladies' Auxiliary beating my door down, begging me to undress them? No thank you. I have my hands full with you."

"I didn't beat your door down."

Slowly, he peeled the sides of her opened blouse apart, exposing pale skin and a lacy blue bra. He eased a finger inside one cup, lightly stroking her nipple. It pebbled beneath his touch. "You would have if I hadn't gone out to your car."

"I planned to punch you in the face and leave, not let you get me naked."

"Let me, hmm? I can stop any time."

"No. Don't." She caught his wrist before he could withdraw his palm from her breast. Her cheeks dimpled at him, brightening the softly lit room, and for him, the world beyond the bed disappeared. "More touching. Less talking. For the rest of the night, the only words I want to hear from you are 'Do you like this?' and 'Have pity. I'm too tired to keep going.'"

They'd see who'd be begging for mercy.

He knelt over her, his knees on either side of her thighs, taking his time. He had her blouse unbuttoned already, so he went to work on her leggings. She cupped him in the warmth of her hand. His erection jerked in eager response and his lungs fought for air.

"Hey. That isn't fair."

"Did I say you could speak?" she demanded, squeezing him ever so slightly, just enough to make him forget his own name.

So it was going to be like that.

Game on, baby.

Dan inched stretchy fabric over her hips. Beneath the leggings, she wore a scrap of lace that matched her bra. He trailed his fingertips down the length of her stomach, aiming for that strip of lace. He bent forward, enjoying the sensual stroke of her fingers on him, and eased one of his hands into her panties. He braced his other palm on her belly. With his knees on either side of her thighs, and her leggings only half-off, he had her legs trapped so she couldn't move. He slid the tip of a finger inside her and watched her eyes widen as her hips bucked and she figured it out. He ran his finger over her cleft, again and again, until she was squirming and panting beneath him.

"Do you like this?" he asked.

She nodded.

If she liked being touched, she'd like what was coming next even more. He hooked the tiny panties and the leggings and stripped them off her legs. He debated taking a few extra seconds to get her out of her blouse and bra, but decided against it. Instead, he spread her thighs with his hands, knelt between her bent knees, and let his tongue taste her, making her gasp. Her fingers tangled in his hair as she gripped his head.

"Do you like *this*?" he demanded, pausing for breath.

"Yes," she said.

He cupped his ear, turning his head to the side. "What was that? I couldn't quite hear you."

"Yes!"

He sat back on his heels, ignoring the painful ache in his groin. He wanted her begging. "I'm not so sure... I think you need to give me further instructions."

Alycia, however, wasn't going down without a fight. A stubborn light entered her eyes. "I changed my mind. I want you to touch yourself. Show me how you'd like me to be touching you."

He couldn't hold back a grin. If she planned on playing a game of sexual chicken with him, she'd have to come up with better than that. He had very few inhibitions. He took his length in his hand. Like he'd never done this before...

OK, yes, this was his first time with an audience. And this particular audience only made it hotter for him. Besides, he'd bet money she'd break into laughter before he was anywhere close to coming.

"All I really have to do is run my fist up and down, and I'm happy." He demonstrated, pumping himself a few times while she watched him, her eyes wide midnight pools of intrigued disbelief that only upped his excitement. "Why don't you provide the commentary?" he suggested. "Give me some additional instructions."

"You aren't normal," she said.

He had to admire her self-control. She wanted to laugh but wasn't about to give in. "You said I think like a guy. So what's not normal about me?" he challenged her. "That I can get an erection just by looking at you?"

"Because you can make me laugh and want you so much it hurts—both at the same time," she whispered.

Her words slid straight to his heart. This was one game he had no interest in winning. The victory was hers. He settled his hands on either side of her head, then leaned in for a kiss. She tasted sweet, and soft, and like everything he'd ever desired. She kissed him back, parting her lips and arching against him, the tip of her tongue tangling with his. The scratchy lace of her bra rubbed his bare chest. Her palms stroked the length of his back, then tracked the rounds of his buttocks.

"If you aren't inside me within the next second, I'm finishing without you." She took him in one of her hands, guiding him into position. "I don't want that. I want you with me."

He grabbed a condom and donned it with record speed.

She was so hot and ready for him, her muscles already tensing around his shaft as he made the first thrust, that Dan almost lost it right there. He gritted his teeth, sweat breaking out all over his body. This was her night. It was about her. And he'd be damned if he finished first.

But the soft sounds—the tiny moans of pleasure she breathed against his throat—made his good intentions next to impossible to keep. She arched her back, then stiffened, her fingertips scrabbling against his straining shoulders. He thrust harder, and deeper, and when she cried out his name, her body clenching him with tight, pulsating spasms, his own orgasm erupted.

Afterward, when the world had righted itself, he held her in his arms.

The moon created crazy cobwebs of shadow along the wall and the ceiling. He thought she was asleep, but she rolled into him, thrusting one knee between his thighs and pressing her cheek into the crook of his throat.

"Are you sure you don't want me to go home?" she asked, her quiet voice filled with gentle understanding.

He buried his face in the sweet scent of her hair. Of course she understood. She'd been there herself. But he'd finally worked through his problem, and right now, he didn't smell any roses. "Have you heard me say, 'Have pity. I'm too tired to keep going' yet? That's the last thing I want."

He meant every word. He didn't know where the future might take them. At that moment, however, they were content with where they were in their lives. He couldn't see any reason why they shouldn't enjoy that contentment together, as long as they didn't get in each other's way.

CHAPTER THIRTEEN

"IT'S TIME TO GET up, Bossy Pants."

The blinds shot to the top of the window with a clatter. Bright sunlight streamed into the room. Alycia muttered a rude word and pulled the pillow over her head, trying to block out Dan and his cheerfulness along with the sun, but he was persistent. The next thing she knew he'd grabbed the blankets and was shaking them. Hard. When that didn't work, he went for the underarms. He sat on her and began tickling, tangling her in the sheets and pinning her down so she couldn't escape.

"Have pity! I'm too tired to keep going!" she shrieked, flailing her arms in a mad attempt to dislodge him. "It's a Saturday, you kept me up most of the night, and I'm not a morning person!"

Dan flopped on the bed, making her bounce. "I've got news for you. The morning's long gone. I've been up for hours and I already showered. You sleep like the dead. I even held a mirror under your nose to make sure you were still breathing. You can forget about breakfast, and if you expect lunch, you'd better get moving. I'm starved."

She got her elbows beneath her and propped herself up. She swiped her mussed hair out of her face and blinked against the blinding white light pouring through the sloped gable window. "What time is it?"

"Almost twelve thirty."

She didn't believe it. He had to be lying. She twisted around, trying to get a look at the clock beside the bed. 12:27.

"Oh my God. I never sleep in this late." She'd made more than one walk of shame in her life, but having to do so at this time of day was a new one for her. She threw back the bedspread, then grabbed it and jerked it up to her chin, flustered and disorientated. She was stark naked. "Why didn't you wake me?"

His lean face held humor and a faint hint of lust. "I tried to kiss you at nine o'clock. You told me to get lost, so I did."

She had a hazy recollection of trying to brush something away from her cheek. She rubbed the sleep from her eyes and tried to clear the cobwebs from her head. "This is so awkward."

"Why?"

Because he'd shaved, his hair was combed, and he looked good—really good, so scruffy and sexy—while the crooked grin gracing the corners of his mouth suggested she was not at her best. She wasn't certain how he felt that she was still here.

"I've already broken our third rule by staying past breakfast," she said.

He shrugged. "I don't recall a discussion about either of us having to clear out at a specific time. The rule was about cooking and keeping a stocked fridge."

"A post-breakfast departure was implied. One of the first rules you brought up was that you didn't want your bathroom cluttered up with girl stuff. There's a limit to how long I can survive without it."

He tugged a lock of her hair. "You can't carry it back and forth in a bag on the weekends?"

He was in a good mood. Not freaked out in the least by her presence. Therapy was doing wonders for him, probably because he was a psychologist himself and already so self-aware. Meanwhile, she was barely awake.

"We should have talked about this more before having our first sleepover," she said. Memories of the previous night flooded back. "I showed up here without an invitation, and I feel like I've taken advantage of the situation."

"The precedent's been set, and it's too late for regrets. The new rule in my house is that you get to stay as long as you like and take advantage of me anytime you want. If that means putting up with a bit of bathroom clutter because you don't know how to pack an overnight bag, then I'll have to suffer."

It was impossible not to be charmed. "Your sacrifice is duly noted. However, my girl stuff and clean clothes are at home. I should go."

Dan didn't move, so neither did she. They looked at each other. If he had any suggestions for how they might spend the remainder of the weekend, he'd better speak up. He didn't get to accuse her of pushing him again.

"I could come with you to your place so you can pack, then bring you back here," he finally said. "I'll take you home tomorrow night."

She read between those lines easily enough. He might not be making commitments, but they'd had a good time last night, finally able to enjoy each other's company with no ghosts between them, and he wasn't ready for it to end.

Neither was she. The sex was fantastic. But they'd agreed on casual. Instead, they were playing a game of relationship chicken. If they weren't careful, someone would get burned.

She slipped her arms around his neck. "What are we doing, Dan? We're not ready for this."

He took her hands and held them above her head, pressed her body into the pillows, and trailed kisses the length of her throat that made her shiver. He touched the tip of his tongue to her collarbone and blew a cool breath on the damp spot he'd made. Her head emptied.

"Don't overthink. Just roll with it. Think *for now*, not *forever*. Spend the weekend with me, Allie," he whispered. "Stay."

She was so tempted, but she didn't want to ruin everything by moving too fast. He'd run out on her before because she'd been too demanding and taken too much for granted. Back then, he'd been the one making all the concessions, and while she didn't intend to do that to him again, she had to protect herself too. "How about if I go home, get my errands done, make sure my fridge is stocked for the morning, and you come over later for dinner?"

"Whatever you'd prefer."

If he was disappointed, she couldn't tell. He could be difficult to read when he chose. Things were so fragile between them.

And yet, when it came to Dan, she could never quite leave things alone. She hadn't forgotten her aunt's warning about letting him loose in her home. He had his own set of ethics and he'd never change, so she wasn't about to be stupid.

"We've gone over the ground rules for when we're at your house. I have a few of my own. Mine are about setting boundaries."

"I'm listening." His breath, warm and minty, along with the slight brush of his lips, tickled her throat.

How was a girl supposed to think?

"I understand that your work involves acquiring information..." she began.

His tongue traced the outer rim of her ear. The smooth cotton sheet slid over her nipples each time he shifted his weight. "I thought we weren't going to talk about business in bed?"

"I'm going to make an exception this once. If you spend the night at my place, I have to be able to trust you. I don't want to worry about you going through my files, looking for information CSIS can barter with. If that's going to be a problem for you, then there can't be any sleepovers in my condo—and that would be a problem for me."

"Why don't we compromise? If you don't leave your work lying around, then I won't go looking for it." He ran his hand up her arm and over her bare shoulder in a full-on bid to distract her.

She pulled her flyaway thoughts back together. He might be smart, and evasion was his wheelhouse, but she wasn't born yesterday. She worked with liars every day. She knew better than to agree to anything someone of Dan's caliber suggested without close examination. "Define 'lying around.'"

His hazel eyes shifted to a pale shade of green. Sunlight caught the flecks of gold around his pupils. He hooked a finger in the bedclothes she clutched to her chest and tried to take a peek underneath. "Laptops in the living room... Papers left out where anyone could find them... That sort of thing."

He was playing with her.

She might not expect him to change, but if this was to work between them, he had to be as respectful of her space as she planned to be of his. She struggled into a sitting position, securing the bedclothes tighter around her. "In other words, I should keep my briefcase locked and my laptop password protected at all times?"

"Give me some credit, Allie. I'm not a thief."

When it came to this game, he was good. If she didn't know better she'd almost believe he was truly offended when in fact, he'd dodged her question. She folded her arms around her bent knees, over the bedspread, and settled in for the show. "Yes you are."

"OK, if viewed through a particular lens, then yes, I suppose I am," he relented. If his tone was any indicator, he was also unrepentant about it.

She tried hard not to smile. "No touching my briefcase or laptop. Those are my only house rules," she said. "Don't make me start carrying a gun again."

"We don't need to swear a blood oath on it, do we?"

"I'll settle for your word that I can trust you."

He gave her a kiss, his expression convincingly grave. "I give you my word, Alycia. You can trust me with anything that's locked up or password-protected."

She gave up. At least she couldn't say she hadn't been warned. Being with him would mean being on a constant red alert, always wondering what was going on in his head. In that regard, he was a challenge. In other ways, he was so easy to be around. He didn't take himself too seriously. He thought of her first. He'd done a striptease for her, and it had been awesome.

Her lungs squeezed out all of her breath, and any urge she'd had to smile disappeared. Who was she kidding? She'd left the one thing she should have password-protected lying around, and now, once again, he owned her heart. Despite knowing better, she was head over heels.

That was her problem, not his.

"Give me an extra hour," she said. "I have to go buy a safe. And then have it bolted to the floor. I'd hate for anyone to think it was just lying around and walk off with it."

He got off the bed, gathered her clothes from the floor, and held them a few inches out of her reach so she had to stretch to retrieve them. The bedclothes slipped. She tugged them back into place.

"I'll make you a sandwich while you get dressed," he said. "I wouldn't want you to leave my place hungry."

Dan went to work on Monday more at peace with himself than he had been in a very long time. Alycia was back in his life, and he planned to do his best to keep her there for as long as possible.

He was going to tell John he'd changed his mind about going back in the field.

Eventually.

But there was no rush.

Midmorning, John summoned him into his office.

Dan had to pass the administrative assistant's desk on his way in. Penny was young and perky and a lot smarter than she let on. More than one unsuspecting visitor had given up too much information to her.

"You're very chipper today," she said. "Been to the Greasy Weasel lately?"

"I'm not falling for that," Dan replied. He patted her desk without slowing down. "I'll say yes, then you'll ask me what her name is, and the next thing I know, the entire office will be gossiping about my private life."

"I doubt it. It's a well-known fact that you have no life to gossip about."

"Let's keep that rumor afloat," he shot over his shoulder, closing John's office door on her tinkle of laughter.

"You think she doesn't know you've been to the Weasel with Ms. Evers a few times?" John asked him as he sat down.

"Of course she does. Why do you think she brought it up?" Dan should never have made that comment about stroking himself when Darren, Bruno's bartender, could overhear him. That was gold—too good for Darren to keep to himself.

"Speaking of Ms. Evers." John tapped his desk's gleaming surface. "The PMO met with the Minister of National Defence late Friday afternoon to lay out the evidence against him. He spent the weekend contacting his buddies in the Senate, trying to drum up support."

Dan wished he could say the news surprised him. Politics was a cesspool. The Senate was Canada's upper house of Parliament, with an historic reputation for being an old boys' club. There were a few women thrown in, most likely to fill an unspoken quota, but only because they knew their proper place. "Did he have any luck?"

John's eyebrows rode up while his lips compressed into a thin line. "What do you think?"

Of course he did. MacKenzie wasn't quite an old boy yet, but he was well on his way. He knew how the game was played. "Do we have a problem?"

"We do." John's jaw muscle worked, indicating he wasn't as composed as he might seem. "Marlies Wiersma's name came up."

"How?" They'd been careful to keep her identity under wraps.

"How else? Someone in the Senate has connections." John's eyes slid toward the top of his desk, lingered, then shot back up to Dan's. "If Bernard Vanderloord is out of the picture, he can't confirm Lies's connection to the transcript we have. Right now she's simply someone who showed up at the embassy in the Netherlands at a questionable time. We can backdate her relationship with Harry and have it begin earlier—claim they managed to keep to themselves. Harry's a quiet man who keeps a low profile. It would work." He drummed his fingers. "We can go one step further. We can set Vanderloord up as a double agent and let word leak out that he was our source."

That would be brilliant—as long as Vanderloord was no longer around to dispute it. Some of that newfound peace Dan was enjoying vanished like a whorl of smoke into a gray sky.

"You want me to call in that favor," Dan said.

"You still OK with it?" John probed.

He knew why John wanted to double-check. Dan was only just back from sick leave and had a few counseling sessions to go.

He was as OK with it as it was possible to be. If he had to choose between one of his intelligence officers and a man who had no qualms about starting wars between countries for personal gain, there was no real decision to make. He didn't care about the Vanderloords of the world.

But he did care about Alycia, and this was one of those instances when their work would come between them if she ever knew what he'd done. Disposing of a human life would never be right in her eyes—not that he would ever discuss it with her at the end of a rough day. It would always be there, however. He'd know it, even if she didn't. Could he live with that?

He'd sworn to her that she could trust him. If she ever found out what he was really capable of, would she continue to see him as someone who at least tried to do the right thing? Would she even want to remain a part of his life?

This was why he was so reluctant to tell John he wanted to stay in Ottawa. When things finally went south between Alycia and him again, he wouldn't be able to stay in the same city with her. He'd need an out.

"Yeah," he said. "Let me make a few phone calls."

He started to stand.

"Wait."

Dan sat back down. The sky outside the window turned gray as cloud cover rolled in. They were due for another spring storm.

"I don't think you were cut out for an office, and it's starting to show," John said.

That seemed harsh. Dan took a great deal of pride in his work, and he never would have pegged John as the type to hold a psychological assessment over one of his staff, especially since Dan had passed his and been cleared for work.

"Whatever happened to my team being the best one you've got?"

"Oh, it is." The ghost of a smile lit John's eyes as he gazed calmly over the wire-framed reading glasses perched low on his nose. "And you're an excellent team leader. But you've been restless for months. Every time you hand out an overseas assignment, you get a look in your eyes that I've seen before. If you still have an interest in fieldwork, I have a proposition for you."

Two hours later, Dan emerged from John's office. He hadn't felt this excited—or conflicted—about a job offer in years.

You'll be completely off the books. You'll get your assignments directly from me. How you complete them will be up to you. You can handpick a team whenever you need one. Or you can work alone. You ask me for money, and I get it for you. No invoices required. No questions asked.

He'd worked alongside black ops often enough to appreciate the honor being bestowed on him, along with the high level of trust. These men and women were truly lawless, chosen because they had a proven ability to get things done—and a strong moral core.

He told John he'd think about it. He wasn't accepting without talking to Alycia first. He'd made that mistake once before, and it had cost him.

He wanted this position so bad he could taste it.

He wanted her too.

He didn't see how he could have both.

Midway through the week, Alycia met up with Dan for dinner at the Greasy Weasel.

She'd called because she couldn't wait until Friday to see him. She wanted to talk to him about the case, and they'd agreed weekends were off-limits for that.

They sat in a booth. She was seething.

"The PMO told MacKenzie to hire a lawyer because the government wouldn't be representing him. And guess who his personal lawyer turns out to be." She'd been warned the minister would be difficult to prosecute, and thought she'd plugged every hole, but this defied all expectations. She could feel the case slipping through her fingers.

For his part, Dan seemed unfazed. "No way."

She plunged on, needing to vent. "David believes

Freeland will cite lawyer and client privilege, which means none of the exchanges of goods Freeland brokered for MacKenzie will be admissible evidence. The first thing Freeland did was call the PPSC and demand a copy of your transcript. He also demanded to know where you got it."

"That's going to be a problem for him," Dan said. "Our source was Bernard Vanderloord, and according to intelligence reports, Vanderloord was found dead in his Amsterdam home two nights ago."

"Are you trying to tell me that Bernard Vanderloord recorded his own conversations—incriminating himself—then turned those recordings over to CSIS, and now he's dead?" Alycia didn't believe any of that for one second. If Vanderloord was the real source, CSIS would have given him up to Public Prosecution in a heartbeat. She leaned on her elbows and rubbed her temples with her fingertips. "I have a headache."

"It gets even better. You didn't hear this from me, but a certain member of parliament has been calling his friends in the Senate, seeking support. He claims CSIS is investigating private citizens on Canadian soil. Can you imagine?"

Alycia looked up. There were so many things she could say. "The nerve. How dare he insinuate CSIS would do such a thing?"

Her sarcasm rolled off him.

"He'll have fun trying to prove it. He's deflecting attention, which means they have a reason to be worried. We have them right where we want them."

When faced with Dan's confidence, much of Alycia's own anger and disappointment faded away. Her suspicions, however, did not. He was up to something. "What are you going to do about Freeland's demands?"

"Nothing. You're going to withdraw the transcript from evidence. Global Affairs will never allow you to use it anyway. Freeland and MacKenzie both know we have it, and more importantly, they know that what's on it is true. The transcript reveals their foreign connections, but with Vanderloord dead and MacKenzie under investigation, that part of their supply chain is currently out of commission. Freeland and MacKenzie are going to be more worried about their domestic connections right now—which would explain why MacKenzie is trying to drum up support in the Senate. He'll want to stall any continued investigation on your part. Using Freeland as his personal lawyer is a really nice touch. These guys are smart." Dan didn't try to hide his admiration.

"One of them is dead," she reminded him.

"Even smart people make mistakes. The other two aren't home free yet either."

"They look like they are to me."

Dan paused as if thinking something over, or maybe weighing the risks before he said anything more. "OK. Here's another free piece of intelligence you didn't get from me. CSIS doesn't care about MacKenzie or Freeland. We're after the supply chain. Not so much the who as the how. You need to get one of them to turn on the other."

"Why would they do that? They're both sitting in a pretty good place right now."

"But they're nervous. My guess is that MacKenzie's your weakest link. Get David to put some pressure on him. Quote a little bit of what's on that transcript and see if he bites."

"I don't know what's on the transcript. The close-lipped SOBs who have it refuse to share."

"I might be able to help you out," Dan said. "I'll give

you the transcript if you give me something in return."

She lifted one eyebrow. "You'd better be asking me for sex in exchange for your information, Agent Hanson. I'm an officer of the law."

He gave her a bold grin with exactly the right combination of confidence and heat. "Take it or leave it, Bossy Pants. Those are my terms."

"The things I'm willing to do for my country." His own sudden willingness to part with that transcript raised some serious questions, however. CSIS was up to something, and Dan knew what it was. She hated being suspicious of him. "What about protecting your sources?"

"Our source no longer needs protection. He's dead. Besides, you're going to withdraw the transcript from evidence once you scare the hell out of MacKenzie, remember?" He picked up his knife and cut into the medium-rare steak on his plate. A thin pool of blood formed, and Alycia's stomach rolled over.

It was too convenient that Bernard Vanderloord—the ex-pat with foreign connections—was CSIS's source. She didn't believe it. But if Vanderloord was on those wiretaps, and he had a strong connection to MacKenzie… Now that he was dead, he couldn't refute CSIS's claims that he'd given the transcript to them. Yes, that would certainly apply pressure to the defense minister. Vanderloord's death had come at a very opportune time. She took a bite of her salad. It might be best not to ask too many questions. Espionage was a dirty game that she wasn't eager to play. She'd leave it to Dan.

As she watched him cut his steak into tiny pieces, she realized he was distracted, not unfazed, as she'd first thought. She hadn't noticed the difference because she'd been so wrapped up in venting about her flailing investigation.

"You've got something on your mind," she said. "Want to talk about it?"

He wiped his mouth with his napkin. His gaze drifted to the bar, where Bruno was in the middle of a disagreement with the bartender. They were in each other's faces, waving their hands, making an entertaining spectacle of themselves that had the pub's patrons in thrall.

Or maybe they were creating a diversion.

"Bruno and Darren are up to something," Dan said, scanning the other tables as if searching for what it might be.

And with that, Alycia lost his attention.

Spies. He was more interested in figuring out what was going on with his friends than continuing their conversation. She speared a forkful of salad, squelching a niggling unease. Whatever was bothering Dan, if she needed to know about it, he'd tell her.

In his own time.

CHAPTER FOURTEEN

ALYCIA HAD FINISHED BRIEFING her supervisor on the information she'd gotten from Dan. They were in her office.

"Can I ask you a question?" His tone suggested that saying no wouldn't stop him, so she nodded. "Are you and the rep from CSIS involved in a personal relationship?"

Someone had squealed. In her head she began compiling a list of prime suspects—her aunt took the top spot, followed closely by David—and then decided it didn't matter. Her immediate supervisor was a gruff former police chief from Newfoundland. He was wiry and bald, with a flat stare that could shrivel the soul of a reptile. And he was fair. When it came to the security of the department, he had a right to know. She wouldn't lie.

"Yes."

"Curious at all as to how I came to find out?"

"A little," she confessed.

"I got a call from the defense minister's personal lawyer. He suggested it might be considered inappropriate, under the circumstances."

Well, well. Dan was right. Someone was nervous.

She'd thought espionage was a dirty game. Politics gave it a run for its money.

"Is it inappropriate?" she asked.

A slight twitch in a facial muscle that curled the corner of his upper lip signified how little he cared. "He was blowing hot air. I don't give a damn what you do on your own time, or who you do it with. I assume you're smart enough to take the proper precautions. If not, you own it. On that note…"

He left.

She popped another antacid and tried to focus on what she was reading, but her eyelids refused to stay open. The stress of the investigation—and the attacks on her relationship with Dan—were getting to her. She was three months overdue for a physical, and since there was no time like the present, she made an appointment for that afternoon. She'd ask for a prescription for the pill while she was at it.

The doctor peppered her with questions before ordering bloodwork. With the tests out of the way, Alycia returned to the office.

And promptly fell asleep at her desk.

"You should put in for a vacation," the admin assistant suggested after startling her awake because she'd missed a meeting. "You look like hell."

The next day, Alycia found out why.

She hung up the phone, still in shock. *Pregnant.*

The doctor estimated she was still less than two months along. That put the timing at close to the first night she and Dan had had sex. But they'd used protection, so she couldn't see how. A dash to the bathroom as soon as she got home from work, and a quick scan of the box, offered the likeliest explanation.

Three years was too long to store condoms.

So much for being smart enough to take the proper precautions. While that wasn't what her supervisor had meant, the result was the same. The blame for this was all hers.

She splashed cold water on her face and took a few deep breaths to get past the shock before curling up on her sofa to stare out over the city and think. But her mind was a blank.

However, it wasn't long before her shock morphed to giddy joy. The grass was growing and the trees were in bloom. She hugged her belly. What a coincidence. So was she. She wanted this baby with a fierce, burning desire. The sleepless nights. The first tooth. The scraped knees. Sloppy kisses and tears. She wanted it all. Would he or she have Dan's eyes and calm, quiet disposition? Or her hair and unpredictable temperament?

Dan. Hysterical laughter bubbled over. Her baby's father was a *spy*. Imagine that on Take Your Child to Work Day.

She came back to reality fast. Her queasy stomach flipped over. What was she going to tell him? *How* could she tell him?

She dismissed the possibility of him walking away and denying any responsibility. That wasn't him. Besides, she had a good job and didn't need any financial support, so it wasn't even an issue. The support she wanted was emotional. That might be the bigger problem for him.

But she didn't want him sticking around out of a false sense of obligation. He had his own life to think of. He'd already expressed a desire to go back in the field, and she wouldn't stand in his way. While she'd never considered becoming a single parent, she wouldn't be the first professional woman to go that route.

No matter what happened next, this was good news,

not bad. She knew all about tragedy, and this wasn't it. This made her happy. She had a new *life* inside her.

She was lost in a fantasy about turning her home office into a nursery—she was choosing paint colors in her head—when she heard Dan at the door. He knocked first to politely announce his arrival, but she'd given him a spare key and the lock rattled as he let himself in. A quick check of the clock said it was time for dinner already, and she was still dressed in yoga pants and a long-sleeved yellow T-shirt.

Reality jolted her back to the present. She had to tell him, but the timing had to be right, because if his first reaction wasn't one of pure bliss, she didn't think she could ever forgive him—and that wasn't fair. She needed to get her hormones and expectations under better control before she lobbed him this bomb.

"I take it you want to eat in," he said when he saw her.

She eyeballed his jeans and cable-knit sweater. "As opposed to another night of fine dining at the Greasy Weasel you've obviously planned?"

He dropped onto the sofa beside her and leaned in to give her a kiss. His eyes were warm. "What can I say? I treat my lady right."

She wasn't his lady. Pain over that poked at her heart. Yesterday, she wouldn't have minded. At least not very much. But the news she'd received, along with her hormones running rampant, left her feeling so...

Alone.

On the heels of that realization came another dizzying, hormonal spiral she might as well learn to accept. The next seven months were going to be long ones.

"Hey," he said, spotting the moisture at the corners of her eyes. "If you feel this strongly about the food at the

Weasel, we don't have to order take-out from there either. You could always cook."

"In your dreams," she replied. He was trying to get her to smile by making fun of her cooking, but he was only making it worse, because it was a skill she'd have to improve on. A baby couldn't survive on Dragon's Breath Burgers and french fries.

Talk of food was making her hungry though, and caught up in another hormone-driven spiral, she suddenly wanted a burger. Desperately. With one of those giant, kosher garlic pickles on the side.

Spending an entire evening with him here, in private, was a bad idea anyway. She'd blurt out the news of the baby for sure, and neither one of them was ready for that conversation. She patted his thigh. "I love the Weasel. Let me put on my favorite cocktail dress and the string of pearls my grandmother left me in her will while you make reservations. Be sure and ask for a table on the lanai."

Dan grabbed her hand and pulled her back down beside him. "We need to talk first and I'd rather do it here, not at the Weasel. You know how nosy Bruno can be."

She felt dizzy. The familiar hot, crawling sensation began in her chest. For one split second, she thought Dan must have found out about the baby.

And then she calmed down. The crawls went away. Thanks to rampaging hormones, she was overreacting. He couldn't possibly know. She'd only just found out about the baby herself.

He was a spy, not a psychic.

The panic that flickered across Alycia's face before she

wrestled it into submission didn't bode well for this conversation, but Dan couldn't keep the job offer from her any longer. He had to give John an answer.

In a perfect world, if it came down to a choice between black ops and Alycia, there'd be no contest. The problem was that the offer from John came too soon into this uncertain relationship of theirs for him to be confident that declining it was the right decision. He didn't know where things stood between them. He hoped her reaction would shed more light on it.

"John offered me a new job," he said, plunging in. "It would involve travel."

"You've already talked to him about going back in the field?"

"He spoke to me. The position would be off the books."

Her blue eyes went wide—two clear, brilliant jewels against a backdrop of pale skin and cherry-red hair. "Black ops?"

"I haven't accepted."

But he hadn't turned it down either, and it hung like a lead weight between them. The heating system kicked in with a rattle and sigh. First cool air, then warm, flowed over his head before striking the window behind the sofa where they were sitting. So far there was no explosion from her, but she had to have some sort of opinion.

"If you really want it, you should take it," she said.

"That's it? I should take it? You have no other opinion than that?" Of all the responses he'd expected from her, calm acceptance wasn't at the top of the list.

She placed one hand on his stomach. Heat seeped through his sweater. "We agreed to put our careers first. I knew fieldwork was a possibility for you. I'm not thrilled with the idea of black ops, but that's your decision to make, not mine."

"You get to have a say, Alycia."

She sat up straight so that she faced him, with one foot braced on the floor and the other leg bent beneath her. "It's dangerous. I get it. Do I like that? Hell no. But do I believe you can do it? That you'll make wise decisions and keep the risks to your personal safety—and the safety of others—to an absolute minimum? Then that answer is an absolute yes. I'm not going to make this decision for you. If you want the job, you should take it."

"What about you and me?"

"We're sleeping together. That's it. Things could go downhill fast."

He didn't get it. Something wasn't quite right, but he couldn't put his finger on it. Or maybe he was simply pissed that she didn't seem to care if he stayed or went.

That was it. She was being far too indifferent. This wasn't the woman he knew. Last time she'd been furious, this time she couldn't care less. He'd agonized over how to tell her and this was all the reaction he got. His ego deflated. It was possible she didn't want to get any more deeply involved with him. Maybe it was a matter of self-preservation. If so, whose fault was that?

"I'm glad you're taking it so well," he said. "I was worried you might not like it, and I want you to be happy."

She cupped his face between her palms. Eyes the color of African violets peered into his. Their noses were almost touching. "I want the same thing for you. Do you want this new job?" she asked him again. "Will it make you happy? You haven't given me a straight answer on that yet." Her eyes dared him to lie.

He decided to gamble. He'd make a sacrifice for her

that he'd make for nobody else. She was that important to him. He brushed her lips with his. His decision was made. "I want you more."

It was the truth. He'd do anything for her.

Then, caution and doubt reared their heads. Did she feel the same way about him? Was he throwing an opportunity away, only to have her walk away and leave him with nothing?

"Why can't you have both?" she asked.

That simple question brought him up short. It felt like a test and he had no answer. He'd made up his mind that she'd need all or nothing from him. He eased his arm around her shoulders, bringing her cheek to his chest so that when he bent his head, their gazes connected. The slash of red hair forged a bold statement against the white of his sweater, and his heart flooded with fear.

"Don't do this to me, Dan," she said softly. "Don't make me responsible for your happiness. I'd never do that to you."

Now he got it. God, he was stupid. She was reluctant to get too emotionally invested. He wasn't the only one who was afraid. He had to fix this, and leaving the country right now might not be the best way.

The phone interrupted.

"Let it ring," he said. "It's after six o'clock on a Friday. Whoever it is, they can wait."

She picked up her cell phone from the glass-topped table in front of the sofa and checked the number. "It's David."

"Dammit." The guy's timing sucked, but it was probably important. "You'd better answer. Put him on speaker."

She held the phone out of his reach. "In your dreams. If he wanted to speak to you, he wouldn't be calling me."

"Hey, David," Dan said as she answered, loud enough for him to hear on the other end of the line.

"Yes, that's Dan," Alycia said into the phone, casting him the evil eye. A second later, she stuck her tongue out at him and put the phone on speaker.

David's voice crackled through. "I just got a call from the PMO's office. They're cutting MacKenzie a deal."

"*What?*" Alycia's slight frame vibrated with outrage.

Dan wished he could say he felt the same way. Unfortunately, he had a good idea of what was coming.

"Guess who's going to be our new ambassador to Taiwan."

"They're making him an *ambassador?*"

"It's not a reward," David said. "The Taiwanese aren't interested in having a Canadian ambassador. The position's been vacant for a long time. It's mostly ceremonial and cuts MacKenzie's political career off at the knees."

"Did they say what information he gave up in return?" Dan interrupted. They had to focus on what was important, not what couldn't be changed.

"Enough to save himself and his lawyer buddy. Freeland gets to continue to practice law, but with MacKenzie and Vanderloord out of the picture, he has to use his Ukrainian connections directly if he wants to carry on in the espionage business, and he'd never risk doing that."

Alycia gave Dan another dose of the evil eye as she addressed David. "How do you know all of this?"

"How come you don't? Someone dropped an anonymous, redacted copy of a translated wiretap in my mailbox," David said. "You wouldn't know anything about that would you, Dan?"

"Not a clue," Dan replied. Alycia continued to glare at

him. "Come on, Allie. Don't you check your work mail? Maybe someone didn't know you weren't in the office this afternoon. I'll bet Global Affairs and the PMO's office got copies, too."

"An anonymous document that's been heavily redacted would hardly stand up in court," David said. "It did offer some powerful motivation to the minister, however. He might have mentioned a base commander's name in passing. And confirmation of that Ukrainian information connected to Freeland was gold. My PMO contact said the GAC rep nearly had a stroke when he read it. Anyway. I've got to run. Alycia, you have a great weekend. Dan, you and I should do coffee again sometime soon."

"Bite me," Dan said, and David laughed.

Alycia disconnected the call. She dropkicked a cushion that had fallen from the sofa to the floor. It hit the wall beside the gas fireplace. "I hate losing."

"Why do you think you lost? Just because no one's going to jail?" Dan hauled her onto his lap and pinned her arms to her sides. "Name the last time a politician has done jail time for espionage in this country."

"Fred Rose, 1947. He served four and a half years and had his citizenship revoked."

Someone had brushed up on their history.

"You need to focus on what's important," Dan said. "The main Canadian players are out of commission. We know which countries are outfitting aircraft with nuclear capabilities. Some of those countries are arming drones. We're cutting off their supply chain, both here and abroad. We'll be able to make sure that what's not working in our system—what made the theft possible— gets fixed. We know that at least one Canadian base commander is writing off functional or fixable aircraft parts as decommissioned and putting them up for sale on the black market. Believe me, the military will go after that. And all because you were willing to tackle a case that no one else would have touched. That's the result CSIS was after, and all things considered, the best one you could have hoped for."

"I know," she said. "I don't have to like it. To think of MacKenzie becoming an ambassador for Canada, even if it's not a prime assignment, is so offensive—especially when there are really good, selfless people in the world who don't get any reward out of life."

"Really good, selfless people don't need rewards. They do the right thing because it's the right thing to do."

She twisted around in his arms. "Is that why you want to take the job John offered you? So you can do the right things?"

Dan started to laugh. "I'm not good or selfless."

She didn't laugh with him. Instead, she frowned. "Yes you are. And you're the only one who doesn't seem to know it."

He could have argued it was the excitement, and the rush of adrenaline, that he missed, but he didn't want to. He'd rather she saw him this way instead. It beat the hell out of her non-reaction to his career change.

Not taking this job offer was the right thing to do. It caused him no more than a tiny stitch of regret. She might not want to take responsibility for his happiness, but it was time he took some for hers. He loved her. As long as she wanted him around, he'd be here.

This time, his plans could wait.

He tumbled her onto the floor. "Go grab your coat, Bossy Pants. I have big plans for tonight, but I'm going to have to feed you first. You'll need your strength to keep up."

CHAPTER FIFTEEN

ALYCIA DROVE TO HER aunt's house on Sunday afternoon. Dan had a bedroom floor to install, and she needed someone to talk to other than him. Someone she could trust to give sound advice.

Meredith lived ten minutes away on Pond Street, in a high-end residential area of the city.

Alycia parked in her driveway, sat for a few minutes, then walked the short flagstone path to the door. She stood on the front steps with her fists jammed in her coat pockets, gathering up the courage to knock. She should have had this conversation with Dan first, but she'd seen the thrill in his eyes when he'd brought up that job offer, and she couldn't do it.

Black ops.

If she only had herself to worry about, she'd be better able to deal with it. But she couldn't sit home for days at a time, wondering if she and their child would ever see him again, and worrying about how she'd explain it if something happened to him. She'd have to be strong for two people, and she didn't know if she could do it.

Yet she was wrong to be thinking this way. Dan could look after himself. An army too, if the situation required it. And he'd love every second. If she tried to hold him back, she'd end up watching little bits of him die—day by day, year after year. She couldn't do that, either.

She knocked on the door, her knuckles rapping on cold steel.

Meredith answered in fuzzy slippers and sweatpants, with dirt on her hands. But she was in full makeup as usual, and her spikey, blue-tipped gray hair was as neat and tidy as if she were on her way to the office. She took one look at Alycia's face and her welcoming smile faded.

She held the door open wide. "You'd better come in."

Alycia crossed the threshold into the foyer. Potted plants graced the low windowsills. Long rays of sunshine streamed through the skylight to pool on the stone floor. To the right, a wrought-iron stair railing spiraled to the open second-floor hall. To the left, glass doors enclosed a living room and stone hearth. Beneath the stairs was a small study. Straight ahead was the kitchen with a sunroom attached.

"I take it David told you about the minister's appointment to Taiwan," Meredith said.

Alycia burst into tears. Deep sobs shook through her body. She pressed a hand to her lips.

"You'll have to learn to take disappointment better than this." Meredith patted her shoulder. "You can't win every case, and this one was doomed from the start. Besides, it's better for you this way. It won't negatively impact your career."

"I'm pregnant."

It was the first time she'd said it out loud. She'd been holding it in for almost twenty-four hours and felt as if she'd explode if she didn't.

"I see." Her aunt's face donned a familiar, neutral mask. When they were girls, Alycia and her sister had called it her court face. Behind it, wheels were undoubtedly spinning. "He didn't react well."

Alycia fished a tissue out of her bag and blew her nose. "I haven't told him yet. I've only just found out myself."

"I don't want to sound harsh, sweetheart," Meredith said, "but if that's true, then you should be talking to him, not me. So why are you here instead?"

"Because I don't know how to tell him. He's been offered a position that would involve a lot of travel outside of the country for weeks at a time, and I don't want to ruin it for him."

"And again, I don't want to sound harsh, but military personnel have to leave family behind whenever they're deployed. I don't care if he's CSIS. He's not a special snowflake. He'll survive." Meredith took her by the arm and steered her toward the kitchen. "Come out to the sunroom and help me pot flowers while we talk." She leaned in closer and dropped her voice to a whisper. "Do you want me to make him disappear?"

"I shouldn't have come to you if you can't be serious," Alycia said.

"I'm deadly serious. Not about making him disappear," Meredith amended. "But he doesn't get to dodge responsibility for this. If you think you'll need a lawyer to get child support out of him, I can take care of that."

"I don't need a lawyer. Or child support. I can afford a baby." She set a hand on her stomach. "I *want* this baby." It shocked her how much, since it hadn't even been on her radar. Perhaps it was her approaching birthday—she'd soon be thirty-three, and she'd stopped entertaining the possibility of children after Terry was killed. They'd talked about it, though.

She and Dan had never reached that point. They weren't there now, either.

Meredith's sunroom was warm and smelled of clean earth. Bright lawn furniture had been pushed against one glass-paned wall. Outside, buckets covered with tarps lined the back of the fenced-in garden, waiting for a few warm days in a row so their contents could be replanted.

"Fill these for me." Meredith passed Alycia a stack of clay flower pots and a bag of soil. "I'm not going to pretend I'm happy about who the father is," she continued. "But he has rights. You don't get to make decisions for him. Not about this."

No, Alycia supposed she didn't. Dan had once made a game-changing decision for her, and she'd been enraged. She filled a pot to the underside of the rim and tamped the spongy soil around the edges.

"Mind you, if he makes the wrong decision, we'll revisit my offer to make him disappear." Meredith tucked bulbs into some of the pots she'd already filled, placing the finished pots on a ledge along the base of the wall butting up against the garden. She dusted off her hands, stretched her back, and dropped into a lawn chair. She motioned for Alycia to join her. "Why come to me? What more do you want me to say?"

Alycia settled into a chair and turned her face to the sun, closing her eyes against the bright rays. "I don't know."

"Let's forget about what the intelligence officer might or might not want for a moment. You have a life and a career too, and I hate to be the one to tell you this, but the reality is that a baby is going to slow you down. How would *you* like this situation to play out?"

"I want this baby to have a normal family."

"That's not what I asked."

"I want a normal family, too." There. She'd said it. She wanted the life she and Terry had planned together, and that made her feel worse. Dan wasn't Terry, and she didn't expect him to be. He wouldn't want that kind of life. He'd never fit into it, although for her sake—and the baby's—he might try and pretend.

"Define 'normal' for me," Meredith said.

She wished she hadn't come here. She'd only had twenty-four hours to put any thought into this. Most of those hours had been spent keeping Dan from figuring out something was wrong—which was no easy feat. Therefore, her wishes were hazy. And yes, based on old dreams she'd tucked away a long time ago.

"Two parents home at the end of the day, sharing responsibility for dinner, bath time, and bedtime. Packing lunches for the next day. Weekends together, doing family things. Holidays with our families," she said.

Her aunt looked at her out of the corner of her eye. "That's not likely to happen, June Cleaver. You're involved with James Bond. Your choice, I might add. So what's your compromise? Are you prepared to share custody? He might be gone for weeks at a time, but there'll be plenty of downtime for him as well. CSIS or not, if he's a decent human being at all, he's going to want to spend as much of it as he can with his child."

She'd thought of the time he'd be away, not when he'd be home. "I don't *know*."

"Do you want me to tell you what to do?" Meredith asked. "If so, get in your car and go talk to him about this. You'd both better get your priorities in order. Number one should be this baby. It has two parents, which means a discussion between them is in order."

As much as her aunt loved her, Meredith could only hold her hand and be sympathetic for so long. She'd pulled Alycia back to reality before. It was why Alycia came to her for advice. She cut through the doubts and got straight to the issues that mattered.

"OK." Alycia fetched her bag and coat.

"I have one more question for you," Meredith said. "You don't have to give me an answer, but I want you to give yourself one. He's from your past. Do you love him? Can you see a future together? Or is he a piece of unfinished business that you would have been done with if not for this baby?"

"I love him," Alycia said, without hesitation. She didn't have to think about it. It curled through her, glowing tendrils of warmth that enveloped her heart. "I've loved him from the first moment I met him. He's funny, and kind, and someone you'd want on your side if an apocalypse hit. I'd never trust him with my phone or my laptop—he is what he is—but I'd trust him with my life."

And my heart.

That was something she would never have expected a few short months ago. She'd been too afraid. But it turned out her heart was battered, not broken.

"As long as you know what you're getting into." Meredith sighed. "Bring him over next Sunday for dinner. I want to meet him. Unless, of course, he heads for the hills when you tell him the news."

"He won't," Alycia said.

He'd do the opposite. He'd try to be whatever he thought was best for her and the baby. He'd play a part, and she might never know.

That was what she feared the most, and what her fragile heart couldn't take.

Dan was on his knees in the third bedroom, fitting the last strip of hardwood flooring in place.

The room was small, and it had an awkward shape because of the bend of the roof. He liked the house. It had great bones. Whoever bought it next might want to add a third story to give a growing family more space.

He heard Alycia come through the front door. He'd been expecting her, and listening. She had his passcode for the security system, but this was the first time she'd used it. It gave him a rush—the sensation of her coming home.

He tracked her movements as she came up the stairs, then down the hall. He looked up as she reached the doorway. She leaned against the jamb, her arms folded, all blue eyes, perfect skin, and delicate nose. She wore her hair in a high ponytail, a look he particularly liked.

"I don't suppose you'd consider dressing up as a cheerleader?" he asked.

"That depends. How do you feel about carpenters? Oh, wait." She arched her eyebrows. "You're one step ahead of me. And you're already on your knees, too... I'm so turned on right now."

"Give me thirty seconds and I can be right there with you."

She smiled, but it didn't stretch all the way to those beautiful eyes, and a cold chill crept into his soul. She'd been behaving oddly ever since he'd brought up the job offer. He should tell her he was turning it down.

But the words wouldn't come out.

"The floor looks great," she said.

"Thank you." The soft-pink, cherry flooring really had turned out well. He stood up to admire it from her perspective, wiping his dusty hands on his thighs. He had carpenter kneepads strapped on over his jeans, and he peeled off the Velcro bindings.

"I'm pregnant."

He froze in a bent-over position, the kneepads in one hand, and stared at her. She started to cry.

"Oh, Allie." He tossed the kneepads aside and drew her into his arms. "Don't cry, Bossy Pants. We're in this together."

"Really?" she said, her face burrowed against him. Her voice was muffled by the folds of his shirt. "Do you cry over everything and gag when you smell undercooked meat?"

Pregnant.

He let that sink in. It meant they were having a baby. It was too late to keep his genes to himself. He was about to become a father, whether he liked it or not. The dumbass guy part of him—the latent Neanderthal—slapped him on the back. *Congratulations. Your boys can swim.*

But that would be the wrong thing to say.

She punched him in the kidney with a tightly-bunched fist. She couldn't get any muscle behind it, and was swinging blind, so it lacked any real power. "I can feel your heart racing, you chicken shit."

She was swearing at him—the feminine equivalent of a punch in the face. He didn't dare laugh, no matter how tempting it was. She'd think it was directed at her, and it wasn't. Yes, his heart was racing—with excitement and possibly relief, but not fear. She was having his baby. *His* baby. An announcement to the world that Alycia was his.

Pounding his chest might be going too far.

"Say something, you asshole. The first thing that enters your head."

"I hope it's a girl. You're such delicate flowers."

She rammed her right knee into his inner left thigh. That one he felt, and he winced. He'd forgotten about her police training. But at least she was getting it out of her system. And now he knew why she'd been acting so strangely all weekend.

He cradled her tighter, rocking her gently while she cried it all out, and deeply regretted telling her about the job offer. It had made it much more difficult for her to break her own news to him. She'd had to deal with this alone and that was so wrong.

She finally came up for air, sniffling and wiping her damp face with the soft cuff of her sleeve. "I'm sorry for hitting you. And for swearing. That's the hormones reacting. You jerk."

"Let's go downstairs where we can talk about this." He took her by the shoulders and turned her around, then guided her toward the stairs at the end of the hall with a light touch of his hand.

Her back remained rigid beneath his palm, tight with pent-up tension. His guilt level soared. He'd been distracted about turning down a job offer, while she'd been worried about caring for a new life.

In the kitchen, she sat at the island while he plugged in the kettle. He busied himself making tea, not knowing what else to do, giving her time to pull herself together.

As he was filling the mugs, Liam's dog shot into the back yard with Liam hot on its heels. The boy dove for its collar, caught it, and dragged it away from the bushes. Dan waved at him through the glass door and Liam gave him the finger.

"I really, really hope this baby's a girl," Dan said.

Alycia blew on the surface of her hot tea, the thick mug gripped in both hands. "Your luck's not that good."

He took a stool beside her and leaned across the island to kiss the tip of her reddened nose. "Show's how much you know. My luck is fantastic. I'll let John know first thing tomorrow that he'll have to find someone else."

She set the tea down. "Why would you do that?"

She didn't sound as pleased by the news as he'd expected.

"I'd already decided to turn it down. I thought you'd be happy."

"We agreed that our careers are our priorities. Why would I be happy about you passing up an opportunity that, under different circumstances, you'd accept in a heartbeat?"

He wondered if this was a trick question and he was about to be judged. Or sworn at. "Allie, that was before. Now we'll have someone depending on us. *Both* of us. Black ops isn't a family man's job."

"If this is leading up to a discussion about me staying home and baking cookies after the baby is born, forget it. I'm not giving up my career either."

"Let me start over." How to explain? How to tell her how much he loved her, and what she meant to him, now multiplied by an infinite number? "I put off our future once before, and I've regretted it more than you'll ever know. I want to be someone my child—our child—can be proud of. I want to be there for both of you at night. I want to read bedtime stories and tuck him or her in. I want to play games in the park and watch morning cartoons."

"I want those things too. I've thought about this, Dan. Your taking this new position won't keep either one of us from being good parents. We'll have to tag-team it sometimes, but we can manage."

She was offering him too much. Far more than she should, because it was too tempting for him to resist, but he tried his best. "There'd be travel involved."

"I admit I worried about that. But you'd also have downtime between assignments. Lots of parents have jobs that force them to be away from home for periods of time. Our situation wouldn't be any different."

He rubbed the back of his neck. "Maybe you should tell me what I want, since I seem to be missing the mark."

"Admit it. If not for me and the baby, you would have leaped on that job in a second."

True enough. But he'd do anything for her. *Anything.* "I love working behind a desk too. I'm a terrific team leader."

"You're also a liar. Although I'm positive you're an excellent team leader, which is one reason why John wants you in this new position."

"I want you more. You don't have any idea what black ops entails. You can't imagine the things I might have to do." She didn't know what she'd be getting into, and this time, if he didn't return, she'd have another person to worry about. He couldn't put her through that again.

"Do you think I can't accept that you'll need to make difficult decisions?" The fire left her eyes. She played with her tea. "When I was a new recruit, I took a position with a police force in northern Saskatchewan. Three of us were women. One of them became a good friend. She got called to a domestic violence scene where a boy, fifteen or sixteen years old, had gotten high and out of control. He was huge, all muscle, and his mother got scared. When my friend Trish showed up, he came after her with a tire iron. She shot him three times—in the leg, the arm, and then the chest—because he wouldn't stop. He died from the shot to the chest. He was just a boy, and until that day, he'd never hurt anyone. Trish cried for three days and wanted to quit the force, but if she had, it would have been such a loss. She was good at her job. I told her the same thing I'm telling you—if anyone has to make tough life-and-death decisions, it should be someone who knows the difference between right and wrong."

He stomped on a selfish blossom of hope and ground it under his heel. "I'd be working outside of the law."

"I'd take you and your instincts over the law any day." Alycia sighed. "I couldn't do what you do. I wouldn't want to. I'm too quick to react and yes, I can be too emotional. But you love it, you're good at it, and it serves a purpose. I don't want to stand in your way." She placed a hand on her belly. "This baby is going to love you as much as I do. It won't care what your job is. It's going to know you're amazing—because you are."

Dan heard one thing. "You love me?"

"You have no idea how much." Her eyes shimmered with more tears, and his heart constricted at the thought that he'd put them there. Again. "Sorry. I'm a little emotional these days." She brushed them away and drew a deep, shuddering breath. "But you're used to making decisions alone, and accepting all the responsibility for them, and relationships don't work that way. You don't get to decide what's best for me and the baby. I don't get to, either. We're going to talk about this. We're going to work it out. Tell me how you see our future unfolding together."

He dodged the question, because he had no idea. She'd sprung this on him. He was OK with it, more than he'd thought he would be, but he hadn't had time to process the information.

A baby…

"What if someday I don't come back? What will you do then?" he asked.

"I'll carry on. I've done it before and I'll do it again, only this time I'll have an important reason to." She bit her lip. "What if you spend the next twenty years looking at me and thinking about everything you had to give up, all because I handed you an unreliable condom?"

So that was what had gone wrong. He wasn't sorry, and he didn't want her to be either.

"That will never happen," he said. "I've already spent the past ten years regretting walking away in the first place. I'm not going through that again. And as for the condom... If only all accidents could be so amazing." He took her hand and pulled her from her stool so that she stood between his knees. She offered a token resistance, but he could tell her heart wasn't in it. He wrapped his arms around her, loving her closeness and needing to touch her. "I love you, Allie. And I love our baby already. I'm not giving anything up that I wouldn't be getting back ten times over."

She fidgeted with a button on his shirt. "Take the job, Dan. At least until we see what we're getting into. We can reassess in six or seven months' time."

The compromise was a fair one. Better than he could expect. "Are you really sure about this?"

"Absolutely."

"Want to live together?"

"Not yet. Let's give us a few months." She looked up at the ceiling. "The bedroom with the new flooring might make a great office, though."

"It's yours. I'll even install a lock on the door." In his head, he was drawing up blueprints for how a third level would look. She was used to finer homes than this—not that she'd ever given any indication she cared—but he wanted her to have the best he could offer. He kissed her forehead. "Are you scared, Allie?"

"Terrified," she confessed. "What about you?"

"No. Why should I be?" She loved him. He loved her. He had everything he'd ever wanted and more. *A baby.*

He was getting used to the idea already. Hopefully it would draw more from its mother's gene pool. "No matter what happens, you won't be having this baby alone. I'll be there for the delivery. I promise. Nothing will keep me away."

"I'm not afraid of being alone for the delivery, although I'd be sad if you missed out." He opened his mouth and she held up a hand to cut him off. "Don't you dare suggest we have it recorded. That's not going to happen." She gripped the front of his shirt and leaned in to kiss him. "I'm counting on you to take care of yourself. I'm afraid of us not having enough time together."

"Nobody can guarantee how much time is given to them. We'll make the most of every moment we have." He settled his hands on her hips. "Are you really, really sure about the job?" He couldn't seem to let it go. It would kill him if he took it and it came between them. He really did want her more.

She dug her hands in his hair. "I love you, Dan. This is who you are. I don't want to change you."

He'd made a mistake once and then had to wait for her for years. She wasn't getting away from him now. "I never thought I'd get a second chance with you. Thank you for loving me."

She rested her forehead against his. "You asked me once if we could move forward. This is the start. Can I put my girl stuff in your bathroom?"

"Better yet," Dan said, "we'll put in another one, just for the ladies."

EPILOGUE

DAN SCOOPED SAND OUT of his son's diaper and checked for other unwanted objects.

All clear.

Six-month-old Jake was slathered in sunscreen, meaning he was also coated in a layer of grit. His fine fluff of red hair was hidden beneath a blue sunbonnet, and his hazel eyes were well-protected behind the tiniest pair of sunglasses Dan had ever seen. Alycia had a phobia about over-exposure to the sun. Or she might be trying to turn the kid into a vampire.

She had another six months of maternity leave remaining, so when Dan decided on a last-minute recruitment trip to Cuba, he'd made a family vacation out of it. The two months he'd spent in a northern Jordanian refugee city was the trade-off. He'd earned this for them.

Alycia occupied the beach blanket next to him, lying on her stomach under a gigantic umbrella, wearing a royal-blue bikini that rivaled Jake's sunglasses in the tiny department. The bottom half of it bared most of her firm, round ass to the warm ocean breeze. Dan loved it. So did the group of young men who kept walking past.

She refused to talk about marriage yet, but he was

wearing her down. He'd gotten a ring on her finger—a tear-shaped diamond with a yellow-gold band he'd bought in Dubai—so progress had been made.

Jake started to fuss. His timing was fantastic. Dan's target had just strolled onto the beach and was headed toward the water. She carried a beach tote, so was likely checking the temperature and deciding whether or not to go in.

"Jake and I are going for a swim," Dan said to Alycia.

She waved him off without looking up. Jake wasn't sleeping through the night yet, and traveling had thrown him off schedule, so she was exhausted. Since Dan wanted to spend as much time with his son as he could, he was fine picking up the parenting slack. Alycia had childcare control issues to work out.

He lifted Jake, crooking an elbow around his round belly so he faced outward, and tucking a forearm under his chubby butt—the kid was slippery from all the sunscreen—and carried him to the water's edge. Jake squealed with joy, waving his arms as Dan dangled his toes in the waves.

The pint-sized, curly-haired blonde in the bright red bikini and white bathing suit wrap took immediate notice. Few women could resist this particular bait.

"Cute baby," she said, smiling at Jake.

"Thank you, Major Bishop." Dan plopped Jake on his backside in the water, diaper and all.

Maggie Bishop stiffened, going from a perky young student here on spring break to the extraction expert she was in 0.2 seconds flat. Her gaze sharpened. "Who the hell are you?"

"Dan Hanson. John Carmichael told me I'd find you here." Dan stuck out his hand. "I have a proposition for you."

Maggie stared at him for several long seconds, clearly taking his measure. Jake grabbed at the hem of her bathing suit wrap, either in a bid for attention or because it happened to be within range. The major looked down at him, then up at Dan, and finally reached out and took the hand he offered.

"I'm listening," she said.

THE END

Stay tuned for Maggie and Ric's story, coming 2018

Note To Readers

First of all, thank you so much for picking up Dan and Alycia's story. *Her Spy at Dawn,* the fourth *Spy Games* book, completes the first part of the series. Dan appeared for the first time in the second book, *Her Spy to Hold*, and when he did, I knew he had to have his own story.

In fact, he's about to get his own series.

The next book will belong to Maggie and Ric, but Dan will be driving the main plot. The characters in the new series are going to be much more ruthless. Poor Ric won't know what hit him. He's never met anyone quite like her before.

Disclaimer:

I'm not a spy. I don't even play one on TV. I have, however, worked closely with the military, I had a fairly good security clearance, and my understanding of how to do business in Canada keeps me out of trouble with the Canada Revenue Agency. Let's hope that trend continues.

We Canadians have our own unique culture—one I'm very proud of—and why I chose to write stories that focus more on the politics of spying than the pursuit. That's the area I know best and the one that interests me the most.

We're a nation of peacekeepers, not peacemakers, and are happy to work behind-the-scenes. The next books will continue that philosophy.

Canada also prides itself on its freedom of information policies and public disclosure, and CSIS, Canada's spy agency, isn't exempt. If you read the actual *Canadian Security Intelligence Act*, however, as Isabelle did in the first book, you'll note there's a great deal of ambiguity to their mandate, and my characters have chosen to exploit it. They are spies, after all.

Acknowledgments

I'd like to thank Paul McCabe, Brig.-Gen., Retd and Debbie West Boutilier for their help in getting the politics straight. If any details are wrong, the mistakes are mine.

I'd also like to thank Author E.M.S. for their formatting expertise; Syd Gill of Syd Gill Design for the beautiful cover; and Amanda Bidnall for her amazing editing skills.

Thank you to Roxanne Snopek for being a second set of eyes and a great friend. And of course, a special thanks to Annette Gallant for being my first reader and another great friend. You both keep me on task.

ABOUT THE AUTHOR

Paula Altenburg lives in rural Nova Scotia, Canada, with her husband and two sons. Once a manager in the aerospace industry, she now writes contemporary romance and fantasy fulltime. Visit her at www.paulaaltenburg.com to view more of her work and to sign up for her newsletter. You can also follow her on Twitter @PaulaAltenburg and friend her on Facebook: www.facebook.com/PaulaAltenburgAuthor/.

OTHER CONTEMPORARY ROMANCE
TITLES BY
PAULA ALTENBURG

The complete Spy Games series:
Her Spy to Have—Book One
Her Spy to Hold—Book Two
His Spy at Night—Book Three
Her Spy at Dawn—Book Four

From Tule Publishing:
The Sweetheart Brand series:
Her Sweetheart Brand—Book One
Book Two coming soon

From Entangled Publishing:
Her Secret, His Surprise
Desire by Design

Read on to learn more about the first three books in the
Spy Games series:

HER SPY TO HAVE
BOOK 1, *SPY GAMES*

by Paula Altenburg

THE GAMES ARE ABOUT to begin.

Au pair and ex-pat Isabelle Beausejour has been living abroad for most of her twenty-four years, traveling the world with her irresponsible father. When Isabelle finds herself stranded in Bangkok, with no job, no money, and nowhere to turn, she soon becomes desperate.

Intelligence officer Garrett Downing is on the hunt for military goods that have gone missing. Instead, he finds himself coming to the aid of a young woman with more resourcefulness than common sense.

Isabelle has no choice but to accept a stranger's help in getting back home. Once there, however, as enemies turn into lovers, it soon becomes a game of keeping secrets. Garrett is more than he seems. Isabelle knows more than she's willing to admit. Will she choose loyalty to her father over the love of a man who tells lies for a living?

HER SPY TO HOLD
BOOK 2, *SPY GAMES*

by Paula Altenburg

TWO CAN PLAY THIS particular game.

When software engineer Dr. Irina Glasov's top secret project is compromised, Irina has no one she can trust and only one place to turn.

Intelligence officer Kale Martin is ready to step up to the plate. Finished with his latest assignment, he's all-in to help the reserved but very sexy Dr. Glasov find her man. Getting the brilliant doctor to let down her guard long enough for things to heat up between them quickly becomes a game Kale plays to win.

Irina's not foolish enough to trust her heart to a man who lies for a living, and she knows he's been lying to her. That doesn't mean she's not willing to play along.

Unfortunately, a cyberstalker is playing with her, too. Irina soon has no choice but to put all her faith in Kale, because with a higher priority case unfolding elsewhere, he's left on his own to investigate. Can they work together to figure out who's hacking into her computer before her reputation is ruined?

HIS SPY AT NIGHT
BOOK 3, *SPY GAMES*

by Paula Altenburg

YOU WIN SOME, YOU lose some.

Intelligence officer Marlies Wiersma plays hard and loves harder—sometimes with disastrous results. After falling for a man who wasn't who he pretended to be, Lies is anxious to prove to her boss that she won't make the same mistake twice. She accepts an assignment which pits her against a charming crime lord—and alongside a diplomat with no patience for spy games, particularly feminine ones.

When a national security threat results in Trade Commissioner Harry Jordan harboring a spy in his embassy office, his instincts scream that Lies Wiersma is a woman not to be trusted. The two of them are supposed to be on the same team, but Lies is a little too good at these games for Harry's personal comfort. He's been burned by a woman before.

Harry's reluctance to play along proves to be too much temptation for fun-loving Lies to resist, and once again, she finds herself in over her head with a man. This time, however, he's exactly who he claims to be.

Now Lies has to convince Harry that, no matter who she pretends to be during the day, at night she's all his.

www.ingramcontent.com/pod-product-compliance
Lightning Source LLC
Chambersburg PA
CBHW051246250626
47155CB00009B/3184